TRAPPED IN WONDERLAND

WONDERLAND CHRONICLES
BOOK ONE

FoxTales Press

DANI HOOTS

"One of the deep secrets of life is that all that is really worth the doing is what we do for others."

— Lewis Carroll

C~HAPTER 1

I was falling.

Or at least I thought I was falling. It didn't feel like gravity pulling me down and down but more like something decided it wanted to sweep me off my feet and I sort of was floating and not going in any particular direction. Kind of like in ballet when one of the guys would pick me up real fast—sometimes for the routine, sometimes because they wanted to scare the crap out of me. I *hated* when they did that. I couldn't decide if it was going to make me hurl or if my stomach was, in fact, in my throat.

The problem was it wasn't stopping. *At all.* Not only that, but there were spiraling colors shooting out every which way in the abyss I currently found myself in. At least they were pretty though, mainly soft colors versus the neon colors that a main character would expect in such a situation. Yes, I watched a lot of anime and sci-fi. Don't judge me. Anyway, I made a mental note to paint them later. That is, if I survived.

Oh, I should probably introduce myself. I'm Alice Hughes, or at least that was the name I went by. My real name was Meredith, but I always went by my middle name. *Can you blame me?* Regardless, I'm a freshman at East Salem High School. Go Hunting Owls! At first I thought an owl was stupid for a mascot, but an owl actually attacked a bunch of people in the park in downtown Salem, Oregon. I now appreciated *and feared* owls.

You may be wondering how I got into this mess, how I was falling (and falling and falling), and why I couldn't stop. Honestly, I had no idea and was wondering the same thing. All I could remember was running out of the school, excited as it was a pleasant autumn day, and needing to bike to ballet and practice my splits. Then Kate, my best friend since grade school, asked me if I remembered my ballet shoes from my locker (wasn't the first time I had forgotten them). I slammed my palm to my face and hurried back into the school.

Oh, that's right. I had seen a group of boys open a locker and step inside—ones who just transferred to the district this year. Why the heck anyone would want to move to this school was beyond me unless they were transferring from McKay. Perhaps it was the same kinds of people who disappear into lockers, which defied the laws of physics. Or, at least, I think it did (science wasn't my best subject). Either way, it led me to believe I had eaten some bad mushrooms or something, not that I did such a thing. Then, of course, curiosity got the better of me and I went to see what was up with the locker, and now I found myself falling… and falling… and… falling.

The feeling didn't stop either, and when I looked down, there didn't seem to be an end to the abyss. I supposed that's why they called it an abyss. I glanced around every which way, and honestly, I had no idea which way was up, or which way was down. It left me feeling a bit disoriented, and I prayed that my lunch wouldn't come back for a visit. That would make this situation so much worse.

As I fell—or maybe floated? I decided that was a better description of the situation—as I floated, I wondered if this was what the people in space felt like while experiencing zero gravity. I always marveled at what it would be like in space, though I probably would never find out. That is, unless NASA started hiring artists to man their spacecraft. That would be the day.

"Crap!"

The swirls of color had left, and there was nothing but darkness. I felt a slight tug and came out of whatever interdimensional plane I had been in. I figured that's what it had to have been, especially after watching so much sci-fi series and anime over the years. I had become something of an expert on all matters pertaining to fictional worlds, and if I didn't know better, I was in some kind of strange, alternative world. That or I had hit my head somewhere at school and was knocked out cold and this was all a dream, which really was much more likely. But I wouldn't be careless, just in case. If I saw a pink-haired girl like in an anime, I would run away from her as fast as I could. Pink-haired girls always brought disaster.

Whatever I landed on was soft. I touched it, trying to figure out exactly what it was since I was still surrounded by darkness. I felt around me, curious as to what I had landed on. It felt short, almost like grass. It was not light enough to tell, but I was pretty sure it was grass. I did live in Oregon after all. I took a breath. Yes, it was grass all right. It gave off that aroma of summer.

Well, that was one question answered, but I still had no idea where I was. Blackness surrounded me, and I felt lost, even more lost than that time I took a wrong turn in Portland, leading me away from my seventh-grade field trip group. Thank goodness for cell phones. Speaking of which, I decided to pull mine out and turned on the flashlight function. I hated the dark. It felt like solitude. It felt like nothing could help you escape from the dangers that lurked around. It absorbed everything and made me want to cry. I didn't, but I sure yearned to.

Examining my surroundings a bit closer now that my slight anxiety attack had subsided, I found that it was indeed grass I was standing on. How weird, as this seemed to be some random room like a closet. Why would there be grass inside? The walls were plain and white, and there was nothing else in the room. I focused the light up to see where I could have fallen from, but all I found was a white ceiling. *How was that even possible?* This had to be a dream.

Shining my flashlight around, I noticed a doorknob on one of the walls. The door was so flush to the wall that I couldn't even make it out. I prayed that it was, indeed, a door and not a shower handle like in the movie *Clue*. The things I worried about, I swore.

I headed toward the door, and as I moved forward, I felt something hit me right in the forehead, knocking me back a step.

"Ouch!" I placed my hand over my right eyebrow where it had hit. There was going to be a giant lump there. I just knew it. I shined the flashlight up at it. Sure enough, I missed the only thing in this room: a giant pipe that spanned across the room right in front of the door. Rubbing the slight bruise, I just hoped my luck would get a little better, which seemed unlikely at that point.

I grabbed the doorknob. It was cool and smooth, just like a doorknob should be, so hopefully this was, indeed, a door. Saying a slight prayer, I twisted and pulled inward. It didn't budge. I sighed. It swung out, not in. I always found myself doing that even if there's a sign. I took another deep breath and pushed outward.

It took a second for my eyes to adjust to the bright

light. It stung, just as it always did when the sun came out on a rare autumn morning. And, for some reason, my left eye adjusted faster than my right. I never did figure out why that was. Once both eyes no longer burned, I couldn't believe what I saw. The scenery that lay before me was a city but definitely not the city of Salem that I was familiar with. No, this was something much more magical, like something out of a fairy tale. Or an anime. Had my dream come true at last? Was I now a 2D character?

Giant buildings made of glass and steel towered overhead, disappearing up into the sky so high it seemed like they wouldn't be able to. They weren't the typical straight, rectangular buildings like that of my hometown but spiraled and bulged out each and every way. If an engineer were here, they would be scratching their head. Even my sister, who was majoring in physics, would have no explanation. I had seen nothing like it. It kind of reminded me of the stacks in *Ready Player One*, although these looked a lot nicer.

The buildings closest to me appeared transparent, and I could see everyone who was inside the structure, but much of the unglazed parts were covered in vegetation. Ferns, honeysuckle, ivy, roses; name it and it was there. I gasped at the fact that all this could exist, and it was spectacular. I wished that more cities throughout the world looked like this. It felt so refreshing compared to the normal concrete and brick. The aura relaxed my mind and soul, and I almost forgot I was in another world.

I stepped out onto the street to find that the roads themselves were also covered with grass, just like the room I had left. It was the most beautiful grass that I had ever seen. It was something you would only expect from turf, except it wasn't that disgusting fake stuff. No weeds, no dry spots; perfection. Along with the grass, flowers of all types lined the streets: blue star creeper, cranesbill, primrose, and those were just the ones I recognized.

Looking forward, I found something even stranger. The people here dressed as if they had stepped straight out of *Pride and Prejudice*. The women wore frilly skirts and dresses of all types and colors, both bold and neutral. The men wore suits with large top hats and chains looped from their coat button to their pocket, indicating they were carrying pocket watches. None of this was the typical scenery of little old Salem. It'd be pretty cool though but very doubtful.

I took a few more steps. The grass felt soft under my shoes, and I was afraid I was going to step on some blooming flower. As I glanced to see how others dealt with this problem, I noticed they weren't wearing any shoes. *How peculiar.*

This place also didn't smell like a city. It smelled like a forest or a meadow, no fumes or smog or pollution. My lungs, for once, felt clean, and the fresh air felt so great that I wished my home was the same. I could even smell the roses that were across the street.

The street was busy, people conversing and walking toward their destination. Laughter and voices echoed through the area. I tried to see if I could get a glimpse of the edge of the city but didn't see an end to the madness. I knew I needed to find my way out of here or at least figure out where I was. Then I could find a way back home, that is if this wasn't some silly dream.

Deciding it was best to simply ask a person where I was, I approached a woman in a ruffled pink skirt. Her buttoned-up blouse was a matching pink with white threaded designs of cherry blossoms. Her blond hair was done in tight curls, and she had a headpiece with cherry blossoms weaved into it. She even smelled like cherries.

"Excuse me, miss, can you help me? I think I'm lost."

She turned to face me, and I froze. Her face was shrouded in darkness, like a mask. I couldn't see her eyes or nose, not even her mouth. It was as if light didn't hit her face, and all I could see were the shadows that had consumed her features.

She hurried off, ignoring my question completely. Was it because I stared at her in horror or because she simply didn't want to talk? Or was it obvious that I didn't belong here? Especially since I wasn't wearing anything close to what those around me wore…

Curious, I took another look around. I don't know how I didn't notice it before, but I couldn't see the faces of anyone around me. Had I gone face blind? Or was this some kind of custom of the people here? All I knew was that a cloud of darkness covered their faces, and I couldn't tell any of them apart. Fear, confusion, you name it, I was feeling it all, and all of it told me I should run.

I started running through the crowd. I didn't know why, it just seemed like the thing to do. I shoved past all the faceless people, trying to find an escape. It didn't help that I didn't know where I was or where I needed to go. All I knew was that I wanted to get away from here. Maybe I could find the way to the outside of the city if I traveled in one direction long enough.

The citizens of the city all stared at me as I pushed my way through their groups. At least I think they stared at me. Their heads were turned in my direction, so if they did have eyes, I would presume I was at the center of their attention. It made me shiver that so many eyes were on me, yet I couldn't see any of them. Could they even see me, or was I in complete darkness to them?

It was probably a stupid idea to run, and I should have just calmly tried to figure out what was happening, but all the confusion hit me at once. What if I couldn't find a way home? What if I was stuck here forever? What if something happened to me and my family never found out the truth? Even if my dream was to wake up in a fantasy world, that didn't mean I wanted my family and friends to worry. My heart was beating faster now, and all I could do was try to run away from my worried thoughts.

And that's when I heard someone yelling after me.

"Stop! Stop her! She's an outsider!"

I debated stopping for a moment, especially since I had no idea what I was doing, but then I remembered all the fictional stories with outsiders getting captured and being thrown into prison. That's what always happened, right? I mean, that's what happened to Satan in *The Devil is a Part-Timer!* Besides, they didn't sound like they wanted me to stop and have a spot of tea with them or something. They sounded like I was a criminal and they needed to apprehend me. I didn't want that, so I kept moving forward and didn't slow down.

But of course, that didn't last long. I felt something grab me and pull me into an alleyway far from the major pathway. I tried to scream, but whoever it was put their hand over my mouth.

"Shhh, it's all right," a familiar voice said.

It took a second to register, but I realized who had me wrapped up in his arms. It was Chase, a boy from school who was in a couple of my classes. He was definitely a troublemaker, and it had been his locker that I had seen everyone step through to enter this world. Was he the reason I was there? Or was this a dream? I kept telling myself it was the latter but treated dangers as if they were real. I couldn't be too careful.

"Now I'm going to let go of your mouth. Just promise me you won't scream," he said.

I nodded, feeling better now I had found someone I

knew. I had completely forgotten that I had followed them down into the abyss. Everything was so new and surprising that the main reason I had fallen into this world had completely slipped my mind. Chase removed his hand from my mouth but didn't remove the arm that was wrapped around my stomach, holding me against him. I still couldn't see his face since he was behind me. I wondered why he didn't let go, and I began to get a little nervous again although I could feel my cheeks getting warmer.

"What's going—?"

He placed a finger to my mouth. "Wait for them to pass."

Chase kept us in the shadows of the trees that had grown with the buildings. It was very narrow in the alleyway, almost like some of the passageways in the old Fort Worden naval batteries near Port Townsend, Washington, that my family liked to camp at. I couldn't even see the sky from where I was since the foliage was so thick.

We stayed silent as the men ran past us, not even taking a glance down this way, which made me wonder what was over here that they didn't think to look. Maybe it was haunted, which would be *awesome*. I had always wanted to see a ghost. It would be a lie to say I had never binge-watched *Ghost Hunters* at sleepovers with Kate. She didn't see the appeal, but nevertheless she'd sat next to me for hours during my marathons.

After we were in the clear, Chase let go of me.

"What are you doing here, Alice?" he asked as he leaned against the wall. He had that sly smile that he always seemed to wear at school. He wore a pure black suit, tailed jacket and all, with the black tie loose around his neck. Bizarre but not surprising compared to everything else. Maybe he was just trying to fit in. Other than his attire, something else seemed off. Then I realized what it was.

"Your eyes." I stepped closer to him to examine them. They were yellow with black slivers, like the contacts I had seen at Kumoricon, the nearest anime convention. "They are like a cat's! Are you wearing contacts?"

He rolled his eyes, which looked weird with a cat's eyes. "Yes, yes, I know, and no, I'm not. These are what my eyes look like in my true form. Now answer my question."

I shook my head. "I don't know. I went back into the school, and I saw you guys. You entered your locker. I got curious, so I opened the locker."

"Curiosity killed the cat, Alice." Chase sighed.

"But satisfaction brought it back," I responded. Not many knew the second half of the quote, so I made it my duty to finish it every time I heard someone say it in the typical anticlimactic fashion.

Chase appeared semi-impressed. "Well, well, you have quite a mouth on you for being so quiet at school."

I gave him a look and then shook my head. "Still wasn't my fault I fell in. I wasn't going to go inside. I swear! Something pushed me!"

He raised an eyebrow. "Do you know who it was?"

"No. I didn't see who or what it was. Next thing I knew, I was here." I peered around. It was all a lot to take in. I had found myself in a strange new place—one that I had never seen pictures of before or heard anyone talk about. So I asked the obvious question that had been on my mind ever since coming here. "Where are we?"

"Alice, you're in Wonderland," I heard a voice say behind me.

I turned to find Malcolm standing there along with Davis and Melvin. All of them were also in some of my classes. These were the four boys that I had seen jump into the locker. They each wore some Victorian gear like Chase did, but Malcolm's was a little more extravagant. His was dark green with light green lining and ivy embroidery. He had a burnt-orange top hat with deep violet flowers pinned to one side of it covering his raven-black hair. His light blue eyes stared at me, making my heart beat a little faster. Kate, my BFF, noticed I had the hugest crush on him, but I never admitted it out loud because, well, let's face it—he was completely out of my league.

"You mean the arcade? Is this some new attraction they added in the back?" I asked, referring to the arcade called Wunderland off Market Street. I looked at Davis and Melvin. They didn't say a word but just glanced at each other. He must have meant that. Maybe they got a virtual reality game. I heard they were making great progress with VR in Utah or Idaho or something. As I looked at Melvin and Davis, I noticed Melvin had bunny ears matching his orange hair. I was just about to point them out when Malcolm shook his head and answered my question.

"No, not the arcade. This is the real deal. This is Wonderland."

"I don't understand. You can't possibly be talking about the children's tale, can you?"

"Yes." He peered around as if making sure no one else was nearby. "But you shouldn't be here. It's too dangerous, and you aren't ready."

"Aren't ready for… what?" I began when Melvin and Davis grabbed me, and Malcolm pressed a vial of liquid to my lips. I tried to struggle, not quite sure what the heck he was trying to give me.

"Drink this, Alice. You must go home now and forget everything you saw."

Forcing the drink down my throat, I felt the sweet liquid start to make my body tingle. My vision was getting blurry, and I had no idea why the world felt like it was spinning. How could he do this to me, I wondered. Why couldn't he have just asked?

I shoved him back, but it was too late as the vial was empty. "What the hell did you just give me?"

Before answering, I felt Chase wrap his arms around me and pull me back into the doorway that Malcolm had appeared out of. I let out a slight girly yelp, which

I, of course, immediately regretted.

"Come on, Alice, we're going for a ride!" Chase laughed as we started to travel down and down and down.

Great, the floating feeling all over again. It wasn't like my head wasn't already spinning.

CHAPTER 11

When I opened my eyes, I found my friend Kate standing above me. Her long brown hair was braided back, in contrast to my short blond hair that always seemed messy no matter what I did with it. Kate also always wore jeans and a cute designer top, much nicer than the oil-paint-covered jeans and simple T-shirt I usually wore. Just a note—oil paint doesn't come out of anything. Ever. It even keeps that grease smell to it, which I could still make out even after breathing in paint thinner fumes over the years.

"Alice! Are you all right?" She bent down next to me, her brown eyes wide. I must have really worried her.

I started to sit up and moaned. My head was pounding as if Thor were inside my skull, wielding Mjölnir or something. "Where am I?"

"You're in the school. I waited for you to come back out to your bike, but you never did. I wanted to make sure you got your slippers without getting in trouble since you didn't go through the main entrance as usual."

I believed her. Kate always worried about such things. It wasn't like I really would get into trouble. I was good at talking my way out of any situation with a teacher.

She went on. "I came inside looking for you and found you passed out in the middle of the hallway."

I tried to remember what happened but only found a dark haze in my memory. *Dark haze... Why did that seem familiar?* I couldn't recall anything, only coming back into the school and then everything else was gone. What happened?

"How long was I out?" I asked. So much time seemed like it had passed, as if something had happened, yet it could have only been a minute or two.

"Just a few minutes. I'm glad I found you first. You would have been in big trouble if a teacher found you."

I tried to remember why I had come into the school after hours, then it occurred to me. "Oh no, dance class!" I rushed up, which made my head hurt even more. I fumbled and almost fell back down.

Down...

I grabbed my head as it began to pound even louder. I must have hit my head on something or tripped as I was a bit of a klutz after all, but I didn't feel any bumps on my head.

Kate helped me stay up. "Alice, you can't go to dance. You should go see a nurse. I think you might have a concussion."

I shook my head, which made it hurt worse. Stupid thing to do. "No, I'm fine."

"Well, at least go home. You shouldn't dance in this condition. I can see if my mom will take you home. We still have the bike rack on the back of our car from our weekend trip."

I thought for a moment. She was right. I really shouldn't dance in this state. I would be falling all over the place and end up with more problems, not to mention making other dancers mad for running into them. "Fine. I'll text Becca."

I pulled out my phone and texted my ballet teacher, Becca, as both Kate and I snuck out of the school and headed toward her mom's car.

Hey, Becca, can't make it tonight. Have bad migraine. C u tomorrow.

Kate's mom was waiting for her in the parking lot. She drove a little Mini Cooper Countryman that was a bright blue. I liked to call it Smurfie because, let's be honest, it looked like a big smurf.

I grabbed my bike and hooked it up to the bike rack on Mrs. B.'s car. Her full name was Jenny Benjamin, but I always called her Mrs. B. It's always awkward trying to figure out what to call someone's parents. Luckily she told me what to call her when we first met.

Climbing in the car, I smiled at her. "Thanks, Mrs. B. I appreciate it."

"No problem, Alice. How's your head feeling?" she asked. Apparently Kate had already told her what happened while I was busy hooking up my bike to her car.

"It's all right. Just need some rest."

"Have any idea what happened?" she asked.

"No, I just went into the school, and the next thing I knew, Kate was beside to me, trying to wake me up. I probably tripped or something. Should be fine after some Tylenol."

She turned back and started the car. My iPhone buzzed, and I looked down to find Becca had texted me back.

K. Feel better. C u tomorrow.

"So how has school been this year?" Kate's mom asked as we headed up Lancaster Drive. East Salem High was located at the end of D Street, just behind an old strip mall. It was small, and nothing was ever open. I called it a waste of space, but that was just me. There was a cute dress shop though, and I loved admiring the prom dresses in the shop window.

"School's good." I knew it was the typical evasive teenage answer, but my head was killing me.

"What's your favorite class so far?" Mrs. B. always liked to make small talk. I never minded it, but it felt as if something was squeezing my brain and I would rather just rest, though I would never tell her that.

"Probably Japanese."

"I can't believe that you and Kate are taking Japanese. I know I could never take it. It seems so hard." Mrs. B. went on yet again. This was the sixth time she said it was hard, she couldn't believe it, et cetera.

I wouldn't lie. I was taking it because of all the anime and manga that I read and watched. I grew up watching *Sailor Moon, Trigun, Fruits Basket,* and all the Miyazaki films. I couldn't get enough of the art. It had inspired me to become an artist. I spent most of my nights in my room either drawing or painting whatever came to mind. I enjoyed all kinds and types of art as well, not just manga. I was most fond of oils and watercolors. They were complete opposites to work with as one took a lot of time and could be fixed quite easily, while the other was quicker, more delicate, and was easier to make a mistake. They took different strengths, and I liked practicing with both in order to work on my weaknesses.

What I really loved about painting was that I was able to create a world that was only in my mind. Anything I could come up with, I tried my hardest to represent it on the canvas or on paper. The only limit I had was in my head. It was the greatest feeling in the entire world.

"But you must also enjoy art class as well. Kate says you're really good," Mrs. B. commented. She must have noticed I was off in my own little world. Again.

"Yeah, I do. Right now we're doing portraits in class, so that's fun. I haven't really done much with portraits."

"You really like art, don't you?"

"I do. I love being able to make anything I want. It's like being in a different world in which I can let my mind wander. There's nothing else like it."

"You think you will do it professionally? Go to art school and all that?"

I sighed. I didn't want to think about it right now. It was my dream, yes, but others haven't been that supportive of me. My parents thought art school was a waste of time and money and that I should pick a better career like business or engineering. They said there was no money in art and that it wasn't really work, and many of their friends agreed. It didn't help that I had a sister who was starting medical school, and my other sister was a senior going to major in physics. That and both my parents were CPAs, Certified Public Accountants. None of my family understood anything about art. They only cared about what they considered the real world and nothing about the world of imagination.

"We will see, I guess," I finally answered. I looked over to find Kate staring at me. "What?"

"You know you can do whatever you want," she whispered quietly so her mother wouldn't hear. "You don't have to listen to your parents."

Good ol' Kate had been at my side every time my parents threatened to take away my art supplies or ballet shoes when I got a bad grade. If I got anything less than a B, I was doomed. If I ever had problems with homework, Kate was there helping me. I was thankful for such a brilliant friend.

"I have a while. I just don't want to worry about it."

"Okay." After that serious question, she smacked my arm. "I saw you looking at Malcolm in English. You really like him, don't you?"

Not that again. I swore she made it her job to bug me every chance she could. I smacked her back. "I told you to knock it off. He would never go out with someone like me."

Kate gave me that face, like I was despicable for thinking he wouldn't like me. "Why not? You are awesome and creative. He would be lucky to have you."

I sighed. "Because there's a bunch of girls lined up all the time, trying to get him to take them out, and they always get rejected. I don't want to be one of those girls."

"But if you did get him, think of how crazy you would make them all. It would be so funny!"

"Just forget it. It will never happen."

"Never say never." She smirked, as if she knew something I didn't.

I rolled my eyes. That would be the day: me with one of the most popular boys at school. That would just turn me into the most hated girl in all the classes. At least Kate would still be my friend. I mean, she really was my only real friend, so it wouldn't be much different. Maybe I should try. It wouldn't hurt anything other than my ego.

No, I would never have the guts.

After a while, we made it to my house off Highway 22. Mrs. B. dropped me off, and I pulled my bike off the back of her car. I waved goodbye to them, after they made sure I had my keys this time and unlocked the front door.

No one was home as my parents were still at work and my sister was at racquetball practice. For some reason, Oregon was big into racquetball. It was fun but nothing I would compete in. The ball moved so fast sometimes, and I would just get stuck standing by the wall and wouldn't move enough, as my sister's coach said the one practice I had gone to. He was pretty scary.

I set my things on the dining room table and grabbed the phone to call my mom. Usually I biked to her office after dance practice, so I needed to let her know I didn't feel well and that I had gotten a ride home. I also knew I should call right now before I forgot, which had maybe happened once or twice.

After it rang a few times, she picked up. "Amanda Hughes speaking." She must not have looked at the caller ID again.

"Hi, Mom. It's me. I wasn't feeling well, so Mrs. B. took me home."

"What's wrong, Meredith?"

I hated it when my family used that name. It was my

legal first name, but I never came to like it. It felt too stuffy for me, so I always went by my middle name and made sure teachers knew that before they did roll call in class.

"Just have a bad migraine. Decided not to go to dance," I explained. It wasn't like she really cared about me skipping class as she didn't see the point of ballet other than for exercise. It was so much more than that though.

"All right, thanks for calling. See you later tonight."

I heard her phone click off, and I hung up. I sighed and grabbed my backpack. I needed to relax, and the only way to do that was to paint.

I grabbed my stuff and went to my room. As I stepped inside, I could feel my worries just wash away. Splashes of color filled the area as most of my paintings covered all the walls, and even more canvases were stacked inside the closet. People always wondered why I didn't have that many changes of clothes, and if they ever came into my bedroom, they would understand. I simply didn't have room, and I spent my allowance on other things, like paint. If it wasn't art related, then it was comics, manga, and books that littered the shelves and floor.

I took in all the bright colors I painted with, as I always liked to capture the boldest of subjects, when I caught sight of a painting I did from a year ago. I had used bright greens and blues with neon-red flowers.

I stared at it as if recalling something or someplace.

Why did the smell of fresh-cut grass just come to me? I pondered. It was like a memory that had been repressed.

I shook my head. It must have just been an idea I had for a project. Maybe that was what I should work on next: creating a world made of grass and plants.

Pulling out some old brushes, I got busy. Homework could wait until after dinner.

CHAPTER III

I slammed my locker shut as the first bell rang. I had five minutes to get to class, plenty of time to get there and be able to chat a little with Kate. We both had first-period English. What a splendid way to start the day with English. Though, in reality, was there any class that would be good in the morning? I didn't think so.

Heading toward class, I hurried through the crowd of students who were all trying to get to their seats before the tardy bell went off. I had learned to get through crowds pretty well, as it was almost like a dance: jump over the bags that were left on the floor, step to the side as two friends who acted like they hadn't seen each other in forever even though it had only been a day ran to each other and hugged, duck as the arm of a basketball player punched one of his friends in the shoulder. With some of the things I had to avoid, I swore it was like I was invisible.

Finally reaching English, I found the room to be the same as usual: posters of classic novels littered part of the walls, a newly installed whiteboard in the front, and the professor's desk near the old chalkboard that was covered in the reading lists for each section that Mr. Barnes taught. I wasn't looking forward to the next year when we have to read an even longer list of books of which none were sci-fi or fantasy I might add. I didn't care what he said, Isaac Asimov and J. R. R. Tolkien were classics.

Kate was sitting in the back as she always did. I grabbed a seat next to her and placed my books on the desk. Right now we were reading *Great Expectations* by Charles Dickens. It wasn't my first choice, but it wasn't too bad.

"How are you feeling today?" Kate asked.

"Great, other than I'm exhausted. Sorry I didn't text you back last night. I got in one of my hypnotic states while painting last night and forgot about everything else again. Before I realized it, it was midnight, and I hadn't done any homework. I got done around three. I'm just happy my parents didn't notice my light was on that late. My Global Studies homework probably makes no sense whatsoever, though. I don't even remember what I wrote."

She laughed. "I'll take a look at it during lunch. What did you end up painting?"

Just as the bell rang, I watched as Chase and Davis

hurried into the room. It was strange. For some reason I could picture them in Victorian costumes. It must have been because we were reading *Great Expectations* and I had a vivid imagination, at least that was what my father said. I couldn't help it if I had imaginary friends growing up. It was normal, I think.

Chase and Davis took the two seats in front of us, which was strange since usually they sat across the classroom.

I turned back to Kate and our conversation. "I ended up painting some buildings with flowers all over them. I had a vivid image of it in my mind when I got home."

Davis dropped his books onto the floor. Good thing Mr. Barnes was late as he would have scolded him for being so disrespectful with someone else's property as the school owned all our books.

Chase smacked him in the arm. "Watch it, clumsy."

Davis said nothing but retrieved his books from the floor.

I turned back to Kate. "So that's what I painted."

"That's cool that you can see something clearly in your mind. You're lucky to be so talented."

"I don't know. I love art but my parents don't ever understand it. They don't see it as a career and think it's just a hobby."

Kate put her hand on my back and made one of her "I'll always be at your side" smiles, which always made my chest feel a little warmer. "It's your life, Alice. Do what you want with it."

"Thanks, Kate." I knew she was a great friend and that I probably wouldn't find another person like her. Through thick and thin she had been by my side. I just hoped one day I could do the same for her.

English was dull. We went over *Great Expectations* some more, as there was apparently more written between the lines that we freshmen just couldn't comprehend, at least that was what Mr. Barnes kept saying. He just wished kids these days could appreciate such great literature. I felt like arguing with him every time he said that, but I knew it would be a waste of breath. I also didn't want him to get mad at me and make my grades suffer. Then I would have to deal with my parents thinking I was failing a class all over again.

As class finished and I started to pack up for the next subject, I saw a young boy in the doorway to the hallway. He had the whitest blond hair I had ever seen, pure as snow, but he couldn't have been more than ten years old. He stared at me with his gray eyes.

Everything seemed to stay still as the boy looked at me. I just froze, not able to do anything but watch him. I felt like I was looking at someone who couldn't exist, like a ghost, but I didn't know why.

"Alice, are you okay?" Kate asked.

I blinked and the kid was gone. I nodded toward the doorway. "Did you see him?"

"See who?"

"That little boy." I shook my head. It had to have been my imagination. I hadn't gotten much sleep.

"Never mind. Let's get to class."

Algebra class was next, which, again, didn't make mornings any more fun. Luckily my locker was near the class, so I didn't have to hurry. As I switched out textbooks, I heard Davis's voice from a few lockers down.

"She remembers you guys. We need to do something." His squeaky voice was barely audible over the typical hallway noise.

"That isn't possible. I suppressed those memories myself," Malcolm answered.

I glanced over toward them, wondering what they could be talking about. All their backs faced me.

"Davis isn't lying," Chase added. "I heard her say she could remember buildings covered in plants."

I dropped my math book. They were talking about me. I quickly retrieved it and hurried away, hoping they didn't suspect that I had heard them. I didn't understand why my art concerned them so. I got random images to paint in my mind all the time. Why would the buildings with plants on them matter? Why would they care? What did they think I was remembering? And why wasn't I supposed to remember it?

Math went by as slowly as possible, which was normal. Malcolm was in class, sitting a few rows in front of me. He didn't seem to pay much attention to me, and I wondered if they had actually been talking about me. It was highly unlikely as we never really interacted during the first month of school. They haven't even spoken two words to me this entire time. So why would they care so much if I painted a building with flowers on it?

Next was Global Studies with Mr. Lewis, who always was passionate about whatever he was teaching. Today's lecture was on the Roman conquest. The Empire was a bit crazy, I had to admit, especially Nero and a few others, but they were often victorious.

The other reason I love Global Studies was because I was obsessed with the anime *Hetalia*. It made me very curious about random parts of history and if they were true or not, such as Busby's stoop chair, a haunted chair in England that was said if anyone sat in it, they would soon die. I looked it up. It really was a thing. The only problem with loving the show was when Mr. Lewis told stories about different countries, I had to suppress my laughter in imagining the characters doing whatever he was talking about. Those who have seen the show understand.

Lunch finally came at last. I hurried to the cafeteria with my bento, a Japanese-style lunch box that I loved putting together cute meals in and found a spot to wait for Kate. I never saw the little boy from earlier that morning again. It was strange. He must have been someone's nephew or something.

I pulled out my chopsticks and opened my bento.

Now, one of my quirky hobbies was making artistic bentos. And why not? I loved art, and after going through half a school day, I wanted something at lunch that would cheer me up. Today's theme was pirates. The rice on the bottom portion had seaweed sprawled across it like a treasure map. My two boiled eggs were decorated like a skull. Then I just had some fruit and veggies. I was in a hurry this morning; otherwise, I would have thought something up to design them. I honestly could have slept in a lot more if I didn't do this, but I had been looking forward to working with this theme.

"Whoa, nice bento."

I whipped my head around to find Chase looking over my shoulder.

He smiled as he sat down next to me. "Mind if I join you?"

Since he had already sat beside me, I knew he wasn't going to take no for an answer. And honestly, why would I say no? He was a likable guy from what I could tell. A joker, sure, but he always meant well.

"Sure, why not?"

"Thanks." He pulled out a sandwich. By the smell of it, it had to have been tuna.

I tried to hide the disgusted look I wanted to make. Although I loved Japanese culture, I despised fish. I couldn't help it. I just hated the smell and taste.

"That's all you're going to eat?" I asked.

"All I want so why not?" He took a big bite and smiled. "Nothing beats a tuna sandwich."

"Uh, I can think of some things," I commented as I took a bite of one of my boiled eggs. It was strange talking to him. School had been going for a month now, and I rarely talked to anyone in their group. They seemed to keep their distance from everyone, other than all the girls who chased Malcolm around. They looked as if they were searching for something, but what that was I had no idea.

"So," he started. "I heard you talking about having a vivid image of some buildings…"

My eyes flickered over to him. He was staring at me as I took another bite of my egg. "And I heard you talking to your friends about that. Why is it important? Why do you care?"

He raised an eyebrow and grinned widely. "You were eavesdropping?"

"Weren't you?" I countered.

"Touché." He took another bite of his sandwich. "I was just wondering where you got an idea like that. Buildings of flowers and streets of grass."

I started to reply when it occurred to me I never said anything about streets being grass to Kate. All I told her were about the buildings. There was no way he could know that. "How did you know there were streets of grass?"

His eyes widened. "What?"

"I told Kate that the buildings had flowers on them, not about the grass streets." I watched for his reaction. He just stared at me, looking as if he wanted to punch himself for saying something he shouldn't have. So there was something going on that he wasn't telling me, and it had been me that they were talking about all this time.

Now the better question was why.

"How would you know that Chase?" I asked.

He stayed silent, probably realizing he had said too much and didn't want to dig himself in a bigger hole than he already was in. Too late though, because now I wanted answers.

"Answer me, Chase." I sounded more demanding than I should have, but I really just wanted to know the truth. Something wasn't adding up, and after passing out yesterday, I felt like everything was in a haze, as if my world were spinning around off its axis.

"Is he bothering you? I can make him stop if you wish."

I looked up to find Malcolm standing across from me, his lunch bag a little neater than Chase's crumpled-up bag. I wondered if he also had a tuna sandwich for lunch, which I doubted because no one in their right mind would bring that to school for lunch.

"What's that supposed to mean?" Chase asked, a little snarky, as if he thought Malcolm had really threatened him.

"Well?" he inquired once more. I had totally forgotten about the question he had asked of me.

I shook my head. "No, he's not." But that didn't mean I wasn't mad about Chase not answering my questions. Let's be honest though. I couldn't bring myself to start interrogating Malcolm as well. I was too shy, and I could already feel my cheeks start to redden.

"Good, I would hate to think he was doing otherwise." Malcolm gave Chase a look. Chase stuck his tongue out at him. I laughed. With all the things that had happened, I had almost forgotten about this morning. Maybe one of them knew about that strange kid.

"Hey, random question," I began. "You guys wouldn't happen to know anything about a young boy with white hair, would you? I saw a kid running around earlier and was curious why he was here."

Chase and Malcolm glanced at each other. They knew something, I was sure of it.

"No," Malcolm finally answered. "I wouldn't."

"Probably one of the teachers' kids or something," Chase added.

I nodded even though I knew that it was a lie. "That's what I thought."

Malcolm stood there for a moment longer, then nodded to Chase. "Hey, Chase, remember that meeting we had with Mr. Williams?"

"Yeah. We should get to that. Great talking to you, Alice." Chase stood up quickly and followed Malcolm out, taking his disgusting sandwich with him.

I watched as they left in a hurry, frowning. Mr. Williams was absent today.

CHAPTER IV

"Very good." Becca stopped the recording of the song "Mad World" by Michael Andrews. It would be one of the songs included in the ballet Becca constructed around the theme of dreams. She was awesome like that, and with this being her first ballet she created from scratch, I was extremely excited about it.

"We will go through this one more time, and then you three can practice your hip-hop routine for the pre-ballet performance." She nodded to Val, Rei, and me.

I smiled. Three of us got to perform a hip-hop routine to "See You in My Nightmares" by Kanye West. It was a fun choreography that we all put together one afternoon. Well, it took a few afternoons to clean it up. I would have to jump on Val's back as part of it, so we would need a lot of practice so I didn't fall off or hurt her or nearly pull her pants down again.

As I got ready to do our ballet routine, I saw movement out of the corner of my eye. I looked out at the open door that let in the fresh fall air. It was the boy from earlier, standing across the street, staring at me again. A car passed by in front of him and he vanished.

I blinked a couple of times, not sure what exactly I saw. No one else seemed to have seen the boy as they were still gathering together to start the song.

"Are you ready, Alice?" Val asked. I must have seemed out of it.

I turned to her and smiled. "Yeah, let's do this!"

The music started playing about dreams and dying. Once the song was done, the three of us changed into sneakers and got ready for our hip-hop routine. I was glad I remembered my Nikes as it always looked weird doing hip-hop in ballet slippers. The three of us got in our positions and waited for the music to start.

Class came to an end, and I gathered my things. I was going to ride my bike over to my parents' work off Summer Street, which was only a few blocks away, and the ride wasn't terrible at this time of year. Once November came around, I would either have to wait for them to pick me up or find a ride over. There was no way I would bike in that kind of rain or icy weather.

It only took a few minutes to get there as it was just down the street. I stopped in front of the small old building, hooked my bike to my parents' BMW coup, and entered. There were a few people waiting, as those who filed for extensions needed to file by the fifteenth. And my parents thought I didn't pay attention to the real world. Then it would get calm until the New Year came around. Things would get even more hectic until April.

I took a seat in the lobby and waited for my parents. Pulling out one of the mangas I put in my backpack this morning, I started to read *Oresama Teacher*. Although it wasn't sci-fi or fantasy, I found it to be quite entertaining. I personally would love to have Mr. Saeki as my sensei, but nevertheless, it was fiction.

After about half an hour of reading my manga, my parents were ready to go home. I climbed in the car, starving and excited to have leftover Chinese from Golden Crown that my parents had picked up the night before.

"How was your day, Meredith?" my mom asked as she got into the car. Again, they never called me Alice. It was like the name Alice was connected to my artistic side and they figured if they ignored it, then it would go away.

I buckled my seat belt. "Fine."

My dad started the car and backed up from the parking spot. "Dance too?"

"Yup." It was a simple answer, I knew, but if I went into detail, they would never understand. They didn't think it was an accomplishment when I could perfect a brisé. Or the fact I could dance en pointe.

It was all meaningless fun to them.

"What are you doing this weekend? Are you going to go to Kate's house?" Mom asked.

I thought about it. I didn't have much homework, so going to Kate's would be a good plan. Then I could talk to her about Chase and Malcolm maybe. But then again, she would think it was just because I liked Malcolm when really that wasn't the case. *This time.*

"Probably. I need to call her. I'll do that when I get home."

When we got home, I called Kate, and her mother said I could come over the next day for a sleepover. We decided we would meet at the downtown mall and hang out for a while because that was really the only thing to do in Salem. There were also some fun antique stores downtown that we had fun exploring, especially Engelberg Antiks. Last time we were there we found what looked like a secret society codebook. It was pretty exciting, and I still needed to do some research on what exactly it was. There used to be a haunted doll, but they finally sold it, thank God.

Once I hung up the phone, dinner was ready, or at least the leftovers had been reheated. My sister Lilith was home from racquetball practice as well. She had her own car, a little green Volkswagen Bug, and could drive herself. Once she put away her stuff, we all gathered at the dining table.

"So," Mom began as the clatter of utensils hit the plates except for me since I was the only one who knew how to use chopsticks. "How was your day, Lilith?"

Lilith ran her hands through her long, light brown hair, twisting it back into a ponytail. "It was great, physics was fun, chemistry was great. Eugene is such a great teacher and thinks I can study physics on a scholarship for sure."

Eugene was an interesting teacher at our school. He got away with practically breaking every school code in his lab: allowing food during class, playing music, wearing Crocs… Those Crocs, I swore.

"That would be perfect. Then you can save up your college funds for a house." Mom smiled.

"And I also beat one of the head boys at racquetball today," she added.

"That's great; teach those boys how to play." Dad laughed.

"Coach says I should be able to get top ten in the girls division for state this year. I'm hoping she is right."

"That would be fantastic, dear. We are so proud of you," Mom added. I tried not to cough. They were always proud of her. Her and Edith, our older sister who was in medical school at OHSU in Portland. She came home every once in a while when she had time, mainly to have Mom do her laundry for her.

"Meredith, how did you do on that math test you had earlier this week?" Dad asked.

Crap, they remembered. They always remembered. I poked one of the pot stickers with my chopsticks. "I did okay."

"So an A?"

"More like a B minus," I mumbled.

"B minus?"

Before he could lecture me, I held out my hand. "It's fine. The final will replace the lowest grade. I'll study harder next time. I already talked to the teacher, and he said I shouldn't have any problem getting an A after the semester ends."

My sister leaned over and whispered in my ear, "It's because you spend so much time at dance and painting. If you gave up those useless hobbies of yours, you could spend more time studying."

"At least I have a creative mind," I snapped back. I really shouldn't have said that because I knew it would just encourage her more, but I couldn't help myself. I hated it when she treated my things as hobbies instead of being my passion and what I wanted to do with my life.

She moved back to her spot and rolled her eyes. "If what you do is considered creative. I've seen your work; it's crap."

I slammed my chopsticks down. "Take that back."

"Why? It's the truth."

"Girls, stop arguing." Dad finally interfered. We stopped and went back to eating. I hated my sister. We always got into fights like this, and it was always her judging me and making me feel like crap. She acted like she knew the future and what was good for me. Apparently she knew more about me than I did.

"But she is right," Dad went on. "You should focus on your schoolwork more instead of your little hobbies."

I wanted to scream. Not this again. It was all I needed on top of everything else that was going on at school. I wished for once they could just believe in me. "But that's what I want to do. I want to become an artist."

"Someday, dear, you will learn that there are better careers out there. Then you will thank us for making you study more."

Like that would happen. I finished eating my food in silence, not wanting to draw this fight out again, as it was a reoccurrence in our house, and finally excused myself to my room. I slammed my door closed behind me and wished I could lock it to keep my sister out. I knew she would poke her head in here after a few minutes. She always liked making matters worse.

Just as I predicted, my sister came into the room mere seconds later.

"What do you want?" I asked as I lay on my bed and started reading the next volume of *Oresama Teacher*. I wanted to know more about why Mr. Saeki was so keen on adding students to the school. I always found manga to be a great escape from reality, as I could fall into the world and forget everything my family said to me.

Lilith didn't come any farther into the room than the doorway. "I wasn't joking. You really should focus on better things. Everyone in our family is successful. It would be a shame if you weren't."

I rolled my eyes. "Being successful isn't everything."

"Sure, keep telling yourself that. Just keep in mind what they said. You will thank them later."

"I'll try."

"Hmm, we will see about that. I would say that you should try to fit in, but that is impossible. I mean, how many friends do you even have at school? Just Kate? You know she only hangs out with you because she pities you. Alice, you need to just grow up and act like a normal person."

"Shut up!"

She hurried out the door before the pillow I threw hit her.

CHAPTER V

I woke up to the wind swirling around my room, picking up papers like dry leaves. I moaned as I got up out of bed to shut the window. I swore I had closed it already. I glanced at the clock. It was three a.m. *Seriously?* I needed more sleep in order to function properly. At least I could sleep in the next day, and I was just going to hang out with Kate all day. I couldn't wait. Maybe that was why I woke up so easily.

I shut the window and went back to bed. I put my head down on the pillow and snuggled with my TARDIS blanket. It was so soft. I loved the feel of it against my skin. I wish I could run away from all my problems with the Doctor (ninth Doctor to be exact, but I wasn't picky). Not that it would solve any of my problems, but it would be fun.

"Alice." A whisper came across the room. "Come,

Alice."

I jerked my head up and peered around the room. Nothing moved and there was nowhere anyone could hide in my room, believe me.

"Allllliiiiiice," the sweet voice called.

That time I knew I wasn't imagining it. It sounded like a child's voice. Could it have been the kid I had seen earlier that day? I blinked a few times, trying to concentrate, but I couldn't. Once I heard the voice this time, my mind went into a daze, and I couldn't think clearly. All my mind and body wanted to do was follow the voice. I had to go to the kid. I had to know what he wanted.

I stepped out of my bed, half-aware of what I was doing, half not. It was stupid to follow a voice coming from something you didn't know, especially when it was sweet and eerie. I knew that much from every horror story I ever read. I swore the creepiest stories had kids in it as well. Even with those thoughts going through my head, I couldn't stop. No matter the things my mind screamed at my body, I succumbed to the voice.

Going straight back to the window I had just closed, I slid it open again and climbed outside. Luckily my window went into the front yard and was easy to climb out of. I was afraid of what I might have done if that weren't the case, such as climbing down a drainpipe like people did in the movies.

No one in the house noticed as I snuck off into the

night—in my pajamas no less. I wished whatever this voice was would have ordered me to change into clothes. I mean, what if someone saw me? But then again, I was a zombie and wasn't able to control my body. I felt helpless. It was the worse feeling in the world. At least I had worn socks to bed. It got chilly at night in Oregon.

The autumn leaves crunched under my feet as I left the driveway. The gravel underneath hurt, but the socks kept my feet from getting cut. I should have stopped, but I couldn't. I was under the spell of the person calling me.

"Alice," the voice echoed through the night.

I kept moving down the gravel road, my feet screaming at me in agony. I would definitely be suffering in ballet the next week. At least my feet were tough after all the practice I had in class, but that didn't make the pain any less.

The gravel road was a dead end. I knew that before this zombie-like adventure. I used to sneak out into this forest when I was younger, against my parents' wishes, just so I could get away from the world and dream. I used to think if I ventured out here long enough, I would find fairies or a castle or some fantastical creature that I could share an adventure with. But that never happened, and I eventually stopped sneaking out here. And the fact that Mr. Petrovitsky found me one day and chewed me out for trespassing. He was a very small man, but I swore he must have worked for the

KGB before immigrating here twenty years ago. If he found me tonight, I had no idea what he would do. Probably shoot me.

I stepped into the forest. It was exactly how I remembered it, other than being dark out. Luckily the moon shone down, providing a soft glow, but that didn't mean I could clearly see everything around me. I could make out trees and ferns, but that was about it. I just hoped that there were no wild predators out at this time of the night, as I had heard coyotes howling the other night. God, I wished I could stop.

"Alice…"

Oh right, the voice is what brought me out here. I hoped I could figure out who was calling me. Yes, I figured it was the boy, but that didn't mean I knew exactly who he was. I wanted to know what he wanted but not like this. I had no control over anything I was doing, and it was pitch-black in these woods.

I went deeper and deeper into the forest, and I felt as if I wanted to cry. *Where was the voice leading me? I just wanted to go home. Was that too much to ask?* No matter how hard I screamed in my mind, no matter how much thought I put into it, I couldn't stop my body. All I could think was *why me?*

This had to be a dream, right? I mean, this didn't happen to people. I really hoped that I would wake up and find myself back in my bed and all this was just one big nightmare. But the pain I felt, how detailed everything was, it just felt so real. I doubted it was a dream, but at the same time, all this just couldn't be real.

The forest was calm at this time of night. I didn't see any animals, and the slight breeze brought a rustle through the branches. The bluish light coming from the moon made it seem almost magical. If it weren't so stressful not being able to control my body because of some voice, it would be quite serene.

Then I could see him: the small white-haired boy who had been following me around town. It had been him. I was right.

"It's you," I said. I blinked. I could finally control my body. I stopped walking toward him and looked down at my hands. Yes, I finally had control. "How did you do that? How did you make me come out here?"

"It was quite easy, Alice, as you have a very impressionable heart. All I had to do was call it and you came." The boy stepped closer. He spoke like a gentleman, one way beyond his years. It was strange as I never knew a kid who would speak like that. His eyes met mine, gray as the moon was that night. I couldn't look away. They were almost hypnotic.

"Why? Why me? I don't understand," I said.

"I can't have you spoiling what my master has been planning all this time. You must be disposed of."

He pulled out a gold revolver. I had never seen one like it before, and if I wasn't on the wrong side of it, I would have been quite fascinated by it. On the side of it was a large clock, like an old pocket watch.

"Goodbye, Alice."

My eyes widened and I tried to move my feet, but I was rooted in place. I had no idea if it was because of the boy or if I was just frozen in shock. *Why would such a small boy want to kill me? It made no sense, and who was this master of his? And what plan would I be undoing?*

As he began to pull the trigger, tears formed in my eyes. *Could this really be the end for me, when my life hadn't even started?* I never got to say goodbye to my friends; they would never know what happened to me. I would just be gone. And not even I would know the truth to why.

Just as I thought all hope was lost, a figure jumped out of the trees and on top of the boy. The boy tried to punch away whatever had attacked him, but it was no use. Whoever it was threw the gun away and stood up, his leg pinning the kid down. As he stood up, the moonlight lit up his face. It was Chase.

"Chase, what's going on?" I exclaimed. I hurried to him, able to move once again. It was the worst feeling, not being able to move one's own body.

Chase grabbed my wrist. "No time to explain. We gotta get out of here."

He started running, dragging me behind him. I wanted to stop and ask more questions, but by the sound of it, the boy was back up and had grabbed the gun. I could hear him shooting the revolver at us.

"Don't worry," Chase yelled back at me. "He's a

horrible shot, and I can hear where he'll shoot next. We will be fine."

I didn't understand how he could "hear" where he would shoot next, but I didn't bother to ask for an explanation. Knowing Chase, he wouldn't answer anything just for laughs. For some reason, it felt like déjà vu with him saving me, but I had no idea why. It must have been because of some strange dream a while back.

We delved deeper into the forest. I had never been this deep in the woods before and nothing seemed familiar. Everything appeared darker and more eerie, as if it were possible some witch would appear and try to get us to eat her gingerbread house. Or mushrooms were going to sing to us like in *The 10th Kingdom.* Just as I thought about that, we came upon a small shed or maybe even a house. My heart raced faster, and I knew I would scream if some old lady appeared. Chase ran straight at it. He wasn't even slowing down as we headed toward the closed door.

"Chase, you better slow down!" I tried to pull him back, but he didn't waver. I almost tripped but caught myself and kept running even though I didn't want to. I really had no choice.

He laughed. "Nah, this will be fun, Alice! Just hold on!"

I screamed as he quickly turned around and wrapped his arms around me, still laughing as if he thought this was all fun and games. As he grabbed me, he leaped toward the closed entrance.

And through the door we went. Falling down and down and down.

CHAPTER VI

This feeling—it was so familiar. A black pit of nothing surrounded me, and colors swirled around like paint going down the drain. We kept falling and falling and I wanted to puke, but I restrained myself. There was no doubt in my mind that I had gone through this before. I didn't know what was going on, and my head felt like it was spinning even more than the surrounding colors.

When it all finally stopped, I found myself lying in darkness on top of Chase, as his hands were still wrapped around me. I didn't know what to do; it was awkward lying on him, my face toward his. I felt his hot breath against my cheek. This was the closest I had ever been to a boy, and although I didn't really have feelings for him, my heart began to race.

He let out a brief chuckle. "Are you gonna stay on top of me all day, or are you going to move? I mean,

I'm not complaining, but we do have some things to get done here."

I quickly got up off him, embarrassed I didn't do so earlier. "Sorry, I didn't mean to—"

"Just teasing you, Alice. A lot has happened. I don't blame you for wanting to stay in my arms."

If it wasn't so dark, he would have been able to see the look of me wanting to punch him for saying that and because of how red I was getting. That was not why I didn't get off him. It was because of the shock of the sudden landing. I knew he was joking, but it didn't mean I still didn't want to punch him. I glanced around, the smell of grass filling my nostrils. Grass, that seemed familiar—and not the I'm-from-Oregon-everything-smells-like-grass familiar.

"Where are we?" I asked. Chase didn't answer but got up and headed toward the other side of whatever room we were in. "Chase?"

He slowly opened a door. The light hurt my eyes at first, but then they adjusted and I couldn't believe what I saw.

Buildings covered in flowers surrounded us. It was just like in my painting. My head began to hurt. Pain shot through it like a bolt of lightning.

"Ow, my head."

Chase put his hands on my shoulders. "Everything will be all right. We just have to hurry, okay? Can you trust me enough to do what I ask? I promise I'll soon explain everything. I just have to get you to the person who can help."

I held my head and tried to nod, but the pain was almost overwhelming. I bent down. I had been in a lot of pain before with migraines, but this was beyond overwhelming. I felt like someone was trying to split my head open.

"Hang on, Alice. It will just be for a little longer. You can get past this. I believe in you." He picked me up in his arms. On a normal day I would question this and probably slap him, but there was no way I could walk. I had to let him carry me.

I wrapped my arms around his neck to keep myself steady and leaned my head against his chest. He didn't say a word but started toward whatever our destination was. I wanted to ask more questions, but it was nearly impossible. My head ached to the point where I could hardly think straight.

Chase took me outside, and the bright sun made my eyes and head hurt even worse. The surrounding buildings looked like the ones I painted just the day before. It all seemed so familiar. The roads were even made of grass, just like I had envisioned. The air smelled so sweet, almost like a field of roses.

As for the people, something about them seemed off —other than the fact they were wearing Victorian clothing, though after going to a few conventions, different style clothing never hit me as being peculiar. But as I looked at them, I found that I couldn't see their faces. Some type of shadow covered them like a veil during a funeral. It was quite odd since there was no fabric but only darkness.

Yet it seemed like I had seen it before.

Chase started running through the crowd, no one paying much attention. He definitely had a good hold on me as I didn't feel like I would fall at all. He really should try out for ballet at Tippy Toe since he was strong, and from what I could tell, he had pretty good balance. I told myself to mention that later.

I glanced up at him when I noticed something odd. He had purple hair, like deep purple. I almost didn't notice because of how dark it was. I squinted at the top of his head.

"Chase, why are you wearing cat ears?" I asked. "And your hair is dark purple. When did you change your hair? Are you going to some con?"

"Don't worry about it, Alice. Not important right now."

I closed my eyes and placed my head on his shoulder. I felt him laugh a little.

He kept carrying me through the grassy streets. I had no idea how long this would last, but I knew that soon I needed something that would make the pain go away. I wanted to pass out so badly, but I had to know what was going on.

Chase stopped moving, and I opened my eyes to find us in some strange alley. It was rather small, more like a passageway. It was dark in this area, giant trees towering before us against the buildings. We were stopped in front of an old wooden door, rather different from the glass building we had passed before. Chase knocked on it with his foot.

The door opened to reveal someone I actually knew. Davis. He wore a brown suit. It looked good on him. He looked very distinguished.

"Davis, what are you doing here?" I questioned half-dazed.

"What am I doing here?" He pointed at me. "What is *she* doing here, Chase? This is against the rules!"

Chase shoved past him into the building. "I don't follow the rules. That's why I exist. Besides, she needed to be brought here."

"What are you talking about?" Davis squeaked, following Chase around the room.

"I'll explain in a moment." Chase set me down on a couch. I glanced around. The place was quaint, just a living room that had only a few pieces of old leather furniture. There were other doors, but I had no idea what they led to. I presumed maybe the bathroom, kitchen, and bedrooms, but after everything that had happened, normal didn't seem to exist anymore.

Chase turned to Davis. "Where's Malcolm?"

"I'm here." I watched as Malcolm came out of one of the doorways with Melvin. Their eyes widened as they saw me.

Melvin quickly grabbed Chase by the collar. "What have you done?"

"I had to bring her here. My suspicion was correct.

The White Rabbit had found her. He almost killed her," Chase explained as Melvin tightened his grip. He didn't struggle but let Melvin get whatever frustration he had out.

"You can't just stalk a girl; you have any idea how perverted that makes you?" Melvin went on.

I thought about agreeing, as he had a point, but Chase had saved my life because of it. I really couldn't complain.

"If I didn't follow her, she would be dead!" Chase replied.

Malcolm ignored the two of them and knelt down beside me. He pulled out a small cookie and handed it to me. Something about all this seemed familiar. "Alice, you have to eat this. Now."

I grabbed it and, without thinking about it, ate it in one bite. I realized after the fact that eating some strange cookie that a boy handed me wasn't the smartest thing to do. True, I knew him from school, but I didn't know that much about him. My head was hurting so bad already that for some reason I thought it could help.

And I was right.

Memories came rushing back to me, memories that I didn't know were gone. The locker. This place. Guards chasing after me and Chase and the rest of them coming to my rescue, Malcolm forcing me to drink some potion.

So I had been here before. That was why everything

seemed so familiar. But there were still so many questions that were left unanswered, and now that my headache had subsided, I could finally get these guys to talk.

"Who are you all really? What am I doing here? Who just tried to kill me? What is this place?" Questions spilled out of my mouth.

Malcolm grabbed my hand. "Listen to me. This isn't what was supposed to happen."

I stared at him. He wore that dark green suit I remembered him wearing the day before. His curly, dark hair stuck out from underneath his burnt-orange hat. He looked so handsome that I felt as if I were going to melt when he touched my hand. But I couldn't. I had to figure out what was going on.

I pulled my hand out of his, letting him know he couldn't smooth talk his way out of answering me. "What was supposed to happen? I don't understand."

"You were supposed to be told of this war before coming here. We weren't going to force you into this, but somehow they found out about you. We had to act quickly."

Chase butted in. "You mean *I* had to act quickly?"

Malcolm gave him a look and turned back to me. "Either way, here you are."

"Here I am? Where the hell am I? What is this place? Why are you all wearing weird clothes? And what do you mean tell me of a war? What war?"

He smiled. "So many questions, so curious. But let's

start off with your first one. Alice, this is Wonderland. You are in Wonderland."

I wrinkled my nose, thinking he was just making fun of me. I glanced over at the others, but they didn't seem to be laughing. "You mean… like the kid's book?"

He nodded. "Yes."

"But that's just a story. That isn't real. There's no way."

"It's real, Alice," Chase repeated. "It's all real."

I shook my head. It had to be some elaborate prank. Everyone liked pulling pranks on me since I was so gullible. I wouldn't let them have the pleasure this time. "No, this is just some weird dream. I'll wake up and it will all be over."

"No, Alice, this isn't a dream. Alice Liddell was a real person. She told everything to a certain Lewis Carroll, and he wrote the story down. He warped quite a few things, but this place is real. This is Wonderland."

I shoved him away and stood up. "This is just some trick. You're lying. Tell me the truth!"

"We aren't lying," Melvin added. "And we need your help."

"My help?" That seemed strange. I was just some random girl they grabbed from school. How could they say such a thing? "What would you need my help for?"

Malcolm held out his hand. "It's hard to understand. We have to take you to someone who can explain all this."

I stomped my foot on the ground. It seemed childish,

I knew, but I wanted my answers given to me. This was all just so confusing. "I'm not going anywhere until I understand what's going on."

"Come on, Alice, don't you want an adventure? Don't you dream of such things? I see you reading all those fantasy novels and manga. Now you can live this one out." Chase smiled widely.

I stared at him, and that was when I remembered. "Your eyes! What's wrong with your eyes?"

"Can't you tell?" He disappeared from where he was standing and appeared next to me with his arm around my shoulder. "I'm the Cheshire cat."

I jumped away from him. "What the hell? How did you do that?"

"Chase, did you really have to tell her like that?" Melvin looked annoyed. "You could have scared her out the door."

"Well, she's going to wonder why I look like a cat anyway. Might as well tell her now."

I examined Melvin a little closer. That was when I noticed part of his orange hair seemed off. "Melvin, are those… bunny ears?"

He sighed. "They are *rabbit* ears. Not bunny ears."

Not able to help myself, I reached over and squeezed them.

Melvin jumped back out of my reach and rubbed them. "Ouch! Every time a human comes here, they do that! Why? It's annoying! You don't see me touching your ears all the time."

"But you're human." I kept staring at him, feeling a little bad that I had violated him like that. I just couldn't help myself.

"Nothing is what it seems in Wonderland, Alice." Chase motioned around him. "Nothing is what it is, and everything is what it isn't."

I looked at all four of them with their suits and at the rest of the room. Old wooden desks, leather chairs and couches, bookcases, it was like something straight out of a storybook. It couldn't be possible. Someone had to have been pulling a trick on me. "You're all crazy."

"Well, he is." Malcolm nodded to Chase. "The rest of us are quite sane."

"Ha!" Chase belted. "There is a reason they call you the Mad Hatter, is there not?"

Malcolm sighed and rubbed his temple. "No one has called me that in a long time. They just call me the Hatter."

"The *what*?" There was no way he could be the Mad Hatter. Malcolm was way too young and, not to mention, *sane*.

"Have you not read the story?" Chase asked. "Because you seem surprised by a lot of this."

"I have, but that was written over a century ago. You can't be them. It is a work of fiction."

"Oh, but we are." Chase disappeared and reappeared on the bookcase. "Time means nothing here. We still play our parts one way or another."

I turned to Davis and Melvin. "Then who are these

two?" I looked a little closer at Davis. "And Davis has some weird ears… like a mouse."

"The March Hare and the Dormouse, of course," Chase answered, appearing next to Dormouse, and leaned against him. "Can't you tell a pathetic mouse when you see one?"

Davis's eyes narrowed. "Watch it, Cat."

Chase stepped back. "Oh, I'm so scared. What are you going to do? Throw cheese at me?"

"You two need to knock it off. Alice here is confused, and you two are just making fun of each other," Melvin exclaimed.

Davis turned to Melvin and pointed at Chase. "I'm not the problem here. He is! I have done nothing wrong, so don't blame me."

Chase wrapped his arm around Davis's shoulder. "Oh, stop being such a baby."

They started arguing again, and Malcolm stepped forward, away from the literal cat-and-mouse fight, holding out his hand. "Let's go. We'll take you to someone who can explain everything more clearly."

I looked down at his hand and back to his eyes. Malcolm had honest eyes. I could tell he was someone I could trust, along with everyone else here. I had nothing to lose, really, as I was stuck in this place anyway. If I left them, I would be completely lost.

"Okay, I'll go with you. But first can I get a change of clothes?" I peered at my pajamas. "I don't want to venture around in pajamas if that's okay with you."

"Yeah, pip-squeak here should have something in your size." Chase placed his hand on Davis's shoulder.

"Hey!"

Chase shrugged. "It's true." Dodging Davis's punch, he laughed as he grabbed my hand and pulled me up the stairs.

CHAPTER VIII

Davis's clothes did actually fit me perfectly. He was small compared to the others, but I guess it would make sense since he was the Dormouse. It was weird to wear boy's clothes from someone I hardly knew, especially when he seemed like something out of the 1800s. Don't get me wrong, I loved the era; it was just weird seeing everyone wear such things, except at a con, of course.

I wore a dark pink jacket with brown pants and a purple vest and bow tie. I felt a bit ridiculous in it, as it definitely wasn't something I would ever wear in the real world. It was too fancy for me; I was used to getting paint everywhere, so there was no way I could ever wear this at home. But that didn't matter right now as I wouldn't be painting anytime soon.

Adding the purple hat, I just laughed. This was one strange dream indeed. At least, I hoped it was a dream.

If this was real, it wasn't quite hitting me yet.

I came down the stairs to find all the boys staring up at me. I hated being the center of everyone's attention, especially when everyone looking at me was male. I took a deep breath and smiled.

"Fits perfectly."

"Told ya it would fit." Chase nudged Davis. Davis frowned and crossed his arms, not saying a word in response.

"Well, all in all, you look fabulous, m'lady." Malcolm placed his hand out for mine at the end of the stairs.

I grabbed it, blushing, and took the final step. This was like a dream come true. I recently had dreamed I was going to prom with him, and I was wearing a dress instead of a suit. And we weren't in Wonderland.

"We should be heading to Howard's hideout now since you're already here."

"Who's Howard?" I asked as he led me and the others outside. It was still silent down this passageway, and I began to wonder if anyone else could travel down here; it was Wonderland after all. Maybe they couldn't see it. Perhaps only some could see Wonderland.

"He's the one who knew to bring you here. He's the one who can explain more fully about everything that is going on," Malcolm said.

It wasn't the answer I wanted to hear, but it would do. The promise that someone would explain was good enough for me. Besides, this had to be some kind of dream. There was no way Wonderland really existed. I had probably hit my head while closing my window, and right now I would be on the floor with my face in a plate full of paint.

We walked through the grassy streets. I followed beside Malcolm and Chase. Malcolm had a sort of regal stature about him, honest and true. He seemed like a man who had a high-ranking job, which was weird since he looked like a teenage boy. He looked calm and collected, which was strange given that he was the influence for the Mad Hatter in *Alice's Adventures in Wonderland*. I wondered what happened and what changed him to be calmer and not just recklessly indulging in tea all the time.

Chase, on the other hand, was always a troublemaker at school, and I could tell he was one here as well. I have heard of him starting riots in classes and getting sent to the principal's office time and time again. But his troublemaking saved my life, so I knew I could trust him. I would be stupid not to; he had only been kind to me this entire time. But yeah, he was definitely the Cheshire cat.

Glancing around, I realized that I still couldn't see the other faces. Everyone around me had a dark cloud over their face, like a mask. It was disturbing to say the least.

"Why can't I see their faces?" I asked as we walked past a group of people.

"That's the problem that has shrouded the entire

kingdom. It was why we started looking for you," Malcolm explained.

"Kingdom? You mean the Heart Kingdom?"

Malcolm shook his head. "No, they were destroyed by Alice long ago. The Red and White Kingdoms also fought and destroyed each other. This is the new authority; the Kingdom of Dreams."

I shook my head. "I have never heard of it."

"You wouldn't," Malcolm went on. "It came after the original Alice left. This kingdom is a place where humans' dreams reside. Each person here is a person's dream in your world. This is where they prosper and escape to."

"So then what is the problem? What is the war you mentioned?" Because it sure didn't look like a war was going on. This place seemed perfect other than the weird shadow faces.

"The problem is that the Cirque de Rêves came out of nowhere and started entertaining the citizens—the dreams. We didn't know it at the time, but there is a dark presence controlling the circus, causing the people to become dark and wither away, destroying the dreams of people in the human world."

That definitely sounded like a fantasy. What was this, *Sailor Moon*? Would I be getting Sailor Scout powers? Because that would be cool. I wanted to ask but knew I would sound like a complete otaku if I did.

Because I totally wasn't an otaku or anything…

"That doesn't make sense. So people's dreams in the

real world are being destroyed here?"

He nodded. "Yes, human dreams have always resided here. The more your world grew, the more this world grew as well. Those who keep their dreams at heart stay here, and those who have given up on their dreams vanish from this world and just go on suffering and feeling empty in your world. But it is their own choice to let the dreams escape and crumble. That isn't what is happening. Now the circus is causing the dreams to wither from the inside out. Humans have no control over it in their lives. The repercussions on your world will be tremendous if it isn't stopped."

None of it sounded real. How could that even be possible? I still debated if this was some kind of dream, a dream I would love to express through dance or art. However, there was always the off chance that this was real, that some miracle had occurred, and I was trapped in Wonderland. "How is the circus doing this?"

"They are creating darkness that captures the soul of the dream," Malcolm explained with a bit of a sigh. "We didn't know it until it was too late. It has taken both our queen and king and turned them against those who still have dreams. Only a few of us got out and are trying to stop it before it goes too far."

"Like you all?" I glanced at the others. Each one of them nodded.

Chase winked. "Yes, like us, Alice."

I turned back to Malcolm. "Have you been to this circus?"

A bit of remorse was apparent in his eyes. "Yes."

"Then why aren't you affected?" It seemed like a good question, as these were the few people who didn't have dark shadows across their faces. I wondered what made them so special, other than being in the original story.

He smiled. "The Cirque de Rêves uses fear to get to the soul of dreams. It's how it clouds everyone's minds. He makes you see your darkest fear and lets you live it. It kills the dreams, and they become living nightmares. It didn't work on me though, as I have learned long ago not to live in fear."

I wondered what he meant by that. How could one learn to not live in fear? Even I was afraid of the future, but I tried my hardest not to let go of my dreams. "What about the rest of you?"

Chase raised his hand. "I'm too free-spirited for anything to hold me down. Fear is nothing to a cat like me."

"I have been at the Hatter's side since the beginning," Melvin explained. "So like him, I have learned to live with my fears."

"And as for this mouse here." Chase wrapped his arm around Davis. "He's always afraid, so he doesn't know the difference between fake fear and real fear."

Davis's face turned red. Chase apparently always knew what buttons to push. "Shut up, cat! It's because I'm stronger than most other people around. Only strong people can live in fear and endure it every day."

"Sure it is."

Davis tried to hit Chase, but Chase disappeared and reappeared in front of us, laughing. Davis started chasing him around the group, which was odd to think about how a mouse could chase a cat. It was hopeless though, as Davis could never catch up to him.

I turned my attention back to the surrounding buildings. I noticed that the people, or I guess they were dreams, didn't pay attention to us like they had before when I first came to this place. Was it because of my clothes and I actually blended in now?

There was still a lot I didn't know and a lot I still wanted to understand. I either wished I could be told everything that was going on and why I was needed or just wake up from this very strange dream.

"Why am I here?"

Malcolm let out a brief sigh. "That is very complicated. Howard is really the best man to ask that question. He was the one who sent us to find you. Honestly, we aren't even quite sure why we need you."

"Is he like some kind of mentor or something?"

Chase opened his arms wide. "He's much more than that! He's like a father to us. He has taught us so much over the years and has brought us together to save the kingdom. Something I honestly didn't think was possible, am I right, *Mad* Hatter?"

I turned to Malcolm, but he didn't say a word. His eyes darted in Chase's direction, scowling.

"Geez," Chase said. "Didn't mean to hit a sore spot."

"But yes," Malcolm went on. "He's like our mentor. Even when something seemed impossible or everyone had turned their backs on us, he had been there with open arms. We owe a lot to him, each and every one of us."

I nodded as if I understood, but honestly I didn't. Most adults that I knew didn't think I knew what was good for myself and that art wasn't a suitable career path for any human. The only adult who supported me was Mrs. B., but other than just a few supportive words here and there, it wasn't like I felt I could talk to her about everything. I found these boys to be lucky, but then again, I didn't know the whole story. I learned to never be jealous of someone who appeared to have what you wanted on the outside, because you just never knew what their story was.

"So who is behind this circus?" I asked as the quiet was freaking me out a bit. I always got nervous when it was quiet, which is why people thought I was more social than I really was. Truthfully, I just hated awkward silence. I was usually the one who started making a turtle with my hands.

"A man who calls himself Morpheus," Melvin answered. He looked a bit annoyed at just the thought of him.

I let out a brief laugh. "As in the God of Dreams?"

"You know your Greek mythology well," Malcolm commented.

And the *Matrix*. "I like stories," I explained, a little

excited at the thought of the connection between mythology and this place. "Whether they're ancient. Anyway, to call himself a god, he must be a little full of himself then."

"Is he full of himself? He has converted many citizens as you have seen." Malcolm waved his hand to gesture toward those who stood near us.

I looked around. He was right. There were many people, and I couldn't see any of their faces. I wondered if it was like that everywhere or in just this part of the kingdom. Either way, it was still a lot of people. He had to be strong to be able to convert so many. It was hard to think that the surrounding individuals were the personifications of people's dreams in the real world. I wondered how many around me I actually knew in real life.

"How big is this kingdom?" I asked.

Chase opened up his arms. "It's huge! This is just one section called the Garden District."

"How many districts are there?"

"Within this kingdom? About two dozen," Chase answered. "Most people stay within the kingdom, but there are others who are from outside the kingdom, which is where the ruins of Heart, Red, and White Kingdoms are."

"Two dozen? Wow. Where is the circus?" I didn't see any tents around this area, and this place seemed too strange to have a circus going on.

"In the heart of Wonderland, near the Dark Forest.

They were smart when they figured out how to infiltrate the kingdom—so obviously no one even saw it coming."

That made sense. Sometimes the best place to hide something was right in front of other people's faces. "Which is how the king and queen were affected so fast."

Chase shrugged. "It was more complicated than that, but I don't want to get into the details just yet. Howard will be able to explain more than any of us."

I nodded. "All right, what can you tell me?"

He grinned. "That math test was hard. How did you do on it?"

I shoved him as we made it to the boundary of the Garden District.

CHAPTER VIII

I gasped as we stepped outside the walls of the Garden District. The mountains and forests surrounded the area with trees larger than life. I felt like I was in the redwood forest somehow surrounded by the Alps. I had never seen anything so majestic. I couldn't wait to get back home and paint what I had seen, but I knew I could never bring this scene to justice.

"So where exactly are we going? I mean I know we're going toward where Howard is, but other than that I'm not sure." I stared up at the trees we walked beneath. They were tall, like friggin' tall. I didn't want to know what happened when one of them fell.

It would be loud and destructive, that's what would happen.

"You see where those two hills meet in the distance?" Melvin pointed. I nodded. "That is where we're going."

"And we're walking the entire way?" I asked, hoping that was not the case. I knew it was. I hadn't seen one type of vehicle during the entire time we were walking. Strange, really, but this world wasn't like ours, and maybe they didn't want to draw any attention.

"Yes, we should be there before nightfall." He started down the steep slope, and I followed. Nothing like a good hike after practically no sleep and being dumped into an entirely unfamiliar world. At least I wasn't in my pajamas anymore. Always look on the positive side of things, that was my motto, or at least I tried to make it my motto.

I followed the boys down the slope, slipping and sliding most of the way. The ground was a bit wet, causing a muddy mess. I thought I would definitely fall on my butt. I didn't, thankfully. Nothing new for an Oregon girl though.

I walked behind the rest of them, typical. Although I was good at ballet and balancing, my fear of falling off of something was still substantial. I didn't like the thought of falling and getting my clothes muddy, then having to walk all that way. Walking with muddy, wet clothes was horrible, absolutely *horrible*. So I was more careful than they were, and that made me start to fall behind. And being typical boys, they didn't give a crap about getting dirty. So at least that was the same between this world and my world.

It was still strange to think I was in a different world, that is, if this wasn't just a dream. I think in the back of my mind I really still thought it was a dream, and that was why the freak-out factor hadn't hit me yet. That, or maybe I just watched too much anime, so I didn't find this to be as horrible as a normal person would. Then again, did I truly understand the stakes here? Probably not, but I also had no idea why I was brought here or why some little boy had tried to kill me.

We got to the bottom of the large hill the Garden District was on. As I approached where the rest of the boys were, I noticed they were ducked under the overgrowth, watching something in the distance. Chase grabbed my wrist and pulled me down next to them.

"Careful, they're on the lookout for us," he said in a hushed tone.

I looked toward where they were staring. Five men on horseback were riding across the forest, not too far from where we were. Each was on a dark horse, except one had a white horse. He must have been the leader, as that was how it typically was in the movies. I couldn't get a very good look at many of them, but from what I could tell, they looked like officers for the Dream Kingdom as they were all wearing blue trench coats.

"Who are they?" I asked.

Melvin was the one who answered. "They are the queen's royal guard. The one on the white horse is Bill. He's really good at tracking prey, second best at finding anyone in all the kingdoms."

"Who's the best?"

Malcolm turned and smiled. "Me." He held out his

hand. "Now let's go. We have to hurry if we want to get past him. Chase, come with us. The rest of you go around and hope they follow you instead of us."

Melvin nodded and took Davis with him. They headed around the other way while Malcolm pulled me with him, with Chase just behind us. He seemed a little hesitant at first, as if not wanting to be behind Malcolm or take orders from him. It was barely noticeable, and I wouldn't have thought anything of it, but he didn't let the frown leave his face. Was he mad at Malcolm for some reason? There was a lot I didn't know about this group, but they always had seemed close at school.

Then again, at school, I wouldn't have thought they were all fictional characters.

Malcolm led the two of us the opposite way Davis and Melvin had headed. He took such care in each spot he put his foot that I made sure to step exactly where he did, stop when I was told to, and go on as well. Thank goodness for my ballet classes, otherwise I probably would have lost my balance a few times and fallen flat on my face. That would have been embarrassing.

Chase seemed to be following as well, but he also almost acted like he wanted to go off the path and do his own thing. I just wished he would voice his thoughts instead of holding them in. He must have wanted to stay quiet in case Bill's men were around.

As we came around another tree, Malcolm stopped abruptly.

"What is it?" I whispered.

"He's on to us." He pinched the bridge of his nose. I didn't like how frustrated he looked, as it meant I needed to worry. "Crap, we have to get you out of here." Malcolm searched all around, then finally looked up. "How fast can you climb?"

I blinked. "What?"

He pointed at the tree. "Up. Go."

I looked at the tree that towered beside me and gulped. I had never been good at climbing trees, even small ones. It just wasn't my cup of tea, so to speak. I'd honestly rather dig and hide in a ditch than go up a tree.

Malcolm must have seen the worry on my face as he nodded to Chase and pushed me forward. "Chase, help her. I'll distract them and get them to follow me. Wait until I come back for you. Got that? Do *not* leave this tree unless I say so." He made eye contact. "Do you understand?"

Chase nodded and jumped up to the closest branch with ease, holding out his hand. "Come on, it's easy."

Frowning, I grabbed his hand, and he helped me up the branch. I was already out of my comfort zone and not quite sure what exactly was going on. I didn't need to be made fun of for not knowing how to get up a tree.

At first I was surprised at how well he could navigate the tree, then I realized he was a cat, and it would come with the territory. It was still weird to see his eyes in such a way, but I was getting used to it.

I peered down, which was a colossal mistake, and realized that I, indeed, had a fear of heights. *Or maybe it was a fear of falling?* I started to wobble, but Chase quickly grabbed me.

"Careful, this isn't somewhere you want to miss a step. Long way down."

"Yeah, I see that. Thanks for the tip."

He helped me up higher, and we stopped at the point where we could still almost see the ground but high enough where I wanted to just cling to the tree and never move again. I didn't care for heights, or I guess I didn't care for falling. The latter came with the former.

Chase patted my back. "There, there. Don't worry. I won't let you fall."

"Gee, thanks."

He shrugged and sat down on the branch, cross-legged. "Just trying to help. You need to be like me and not worry about heights. Just land on your feet."

I gave him a skeptical look. Yeah, I definitely could land on my feet, but then I would have a knee coming out of my shoulder blade. I shuddered at the thought of hitting the ground that hard. So gross.

Just as I was about to say something, Chase put out his hand to quiet me. I looked at him with confusion, but then I realized why he didn't want me to say anything. The queen's guards were right under us.

They looked human enough. None seemed to look strange like Chase, not that he looked too different from a normal human being. Bill came on a white horse and searched all around, looking for us. I backed closer to the tree so he couldn't spot me.

I could see his dark brown hair that was slicked back. He wore a blue trench coat, and from what I could tell, he sat straight up as if he had eminent authority over anything and everything. The other four men followed behind, waiting for the man's orders.

"Come out, Hatter, I know you're around here!" Bill's voice boomed through the forest. Chase must have noticed me quiver for he put his arm around me.

"Don't worry, they can't see us," he whispered into my ear.

I nodded, although I found that to be very unlikely. If he was such a superb tracker and was right below our tree, how could he not know we were up there? I tried to calm my thoughts about the situation as I peered back down at Bill.

"Is that a challenge, Bill, or do you know the only way for you to win is for me to give up?" Malcolm's voice answered back. I couldn't find where Malcolm was standing and dared not shift to find out. I just hoped he would be okay, but I trusted him for some reason. Mainly because he had lasted this long and hadn't gotten caught.

"Oh, on the contrary," Bill answered. "I'll find you and that girl you're hiding. Do you really think she can bring down the Cirque de Rêves? Nothing can stop him. You can see that yourself. You are wasting your time!"

"If I'm wasting my time, why are you looking for her? If she poses no threat, stop wasting *your* time."

Bill let out a loud laugh. "You would like me to do

that, wouldn't you? Just because I know I have nothing to worry about doesn't mean that you all aren't being a nuisance. The queen has ordered me to destroy all who are against the Cirque de Rêves, and you, my friend, have betrayed us all."

"You are making a mistake," Malcolm added. It sounded like he was coming from all around. I had no idea where he could be. "The Cirque de Rêves has blinded you. I must stop it before we can never go back."

"We will see about that." I watched as Bill pulled out his gun and started firing into the woods. I jumped at the noise, and Chase squeezed my hand.

"It will be all right," he whispered. "Malcolm knows what he is doing. He has been doing this sort of thing his entire life. And unlike in your world, that is a very long time here."

I nodded as I watched the horses gallop away into the distance after Malcolm. I didn't like the idea of something happening to him because of me. I would never forgive myself even though it wasn't my choice to be there. I still felt as if I could have done something.

Chase and I waited up in the tree for what seemed like an hour. We didn't hear anything from Bill and his men, but neither did we hear from Malcolm or the others yet. I was beginning to worry and wanted to ask Chase what he thought, but I didn't want to make a sound. I had no idea if they were close, and I was afraid of getting caught.

Unlike me, Chase looked calm, his eyes closed and ears attentive. If he was like a cat, he should be able to hear even the slightest noise. I wondered how exactly they worked and how he could have some feline characteristics and some human characteristics.

Suddenly Chase's ears twitched, and his eyes shot open. Then I heard it too, a whistle coming from below us.

"Well." Chase jumped down to a lower branch. "That is our cue."

I smiled as I climbed down behind him. We were finally able to leave this tree and be on our way. I could get answers and stop worrying about Bill capturing us.

I forgot how high up we were until I was almost to the ground. Looking back up, I couldn't even see the branch we were once waiting on. I shuddered. Good thing Chase was with me, or I wouldn't have been able to overcome my fear.

As I thought that, I knew I would jinx myself. It was a curse I had. Even though I was graceful in ballet, I was sometimes quite clumsy in other things. As I stepped on the last branch before getting to the ground, I felt my foot slip and I started to fall backward. I squeezed my eyes shut, waiting for my body to meet with the hard forest floor. I just hoped my head wouldn't hit a rock. That would be the worst. When a couple of seconds went by and nothing happened, I opened my eyes to find myself in Malcolm's arms.

"You should be more careful. We don't want to draw

attention back to us, now do we?" His smile made me blush.

"No," I whispered and straightened back up, dusting off my clothes as I had gotten some bark and dirt all over Davis's clothes he'd let me borrow. I just hoped I wouldn't stain it. "Thank you."

"No problem."

I glanced over at Chase, who was frowning at the entire incident. I wanted to say something, but I had no idea what I could tell him to make him smile again. Whatever was going on between them likely had more to do with each other than the present circumstances. Maybe I would find out about it later even though it wasn't any of my business.

I looked around for Davis and Melvin. "Where are the others?"

"They are already on their way to Howard's." Malcolm nodded deeper into the forest. "We will meet them there. Let's go."

CHAPTER IX

As we approached the edge of the forest, we came upon the once magnificent White and Red Kingdoms. The chess pieces that once stood glorious were now crumbled away with time. They were so huge that they gave the ones in *Harry Potter* a run for their money. The statues and monuments were larger than any building in Salem, but that really wasn't saying much. Salem didn't have any skyscrapers. Heck, they didn't have any buildings higher than 345 feet, and that was the height of the spire at the First United Methodist Church built in 1872. It had been over a hundred years and still no one had built anything higher than that. Salem felt like it was stuck in time, and I wasn't exaggerating. Some of the clothes I saw people wearing on a day-to-day basis were out of fashion long ago.

Then again, I was wearing Victorian-style clothing. I

guess I wasn't one who could talk.

Everything around the area was colored in either red or white decor. It made sense since it was the Red and White Kingdoms. It really stood out, and I couldn't believe that I was standing in a city that had been from a work of fiction.

The ground had red and white tiles, just like a chessboard. If I wasn't there, I would have never believed it. All the buildings were designed like medieval castles with moats in some areas and everything. It was abandoned though, just like they said it was. There were no people in the streets, no voices of conversation. There was nothing but us.

"So this is where your leader is? Was he part of this kingdom?" I asked as we passed yet another moat. I looked down in it and saw something green move around.

Malcolm shook his head. "No, he has been around before the Red and White Kingdoms existed. In fact, he was around before the Heart Kingdom as well. No one knows where he is from; he just comes when he is needed."

"Such as now with the circus?"

"Yes."

So he was the mysterious mentor-type figure, like Obi-Wan or Gandalf. That was pretty cool. "Who is he, in the stories I mean?"

Chase was the one to answer that. "He was known as the Caterpillar."

I remembered that chapter in the story. From what I remember from the book, I always found him rather annoying, and I couldn't believe that he could be such a grand mentor now. "The Caterpillar? I thought in the story he turned into a butterfly or something."

Chase laughed. "The story isn't exact, remember?"

"I see," I lied. I really didn't understand. None of this made sense. "I still don't get why I'm important."

"He had a premonition about you. He told us where to find you so you could help us," Chase whispered so that I only could hear him.

"A what?" I whispered in return. "And why are we whispering?"

"A premonition. A dream, if you will. Those of this world differ from those who represent dreams. He can explain it better than any of us. And I'm whispering because we aren't supposed to tell you anymore until we have arrived."

So that's what it was. Did they know more than they were letting on? Why was it so important that Howard tell me everything? It was obvious that Chase wanted to tell me more, but something was holding him back. Why that was, I had no idea. It would make sense for them to just tell me everything right away so I would understand, but if Howard had more answers than them, I guess talking to him would be a better idea.

I was also curious why Chase seemed to despise Malcolm. I didn't think the Cheshire cat and the Mad Hatter hated each other in the stories. *Did they always, or was it something that happened recently?* As they mentioned, the writer had warped the story I knew. In fact, in the stories I read, Chase had been an actual cat, not part human. I wondered if that fact had to do with Carroll not understanding they were anthropomorphic or if Alice just didn't mention it when returning from Wonderland.

We still hadn't caught sight of Davis and Melvin. I hoped that they were all right and didn't get captured by Bill and his men. I had no idea what kinds of things they would do, if it was like the stories and they would have their heads cut off. But that was the Heart Kingdom, not the Dream Kingdom. Either way I still worried.

"You have nothing to be afraid of, Alice." Malcolm grabbed my hand and kissed it gently. "We will be here with you."

I felt myself blush. Realistically, there wasn't any reason I should trust him or any of the others. They pretty much kidnapped me and brought me here without telling me why they needed me. But for some reason, I felt as if I could trust them. I felt as if this was where I was supposed to be, but that didn't really make any sense. I was somewhere that wasn't supposed to be real. But this world had everything I'd always wanted: an adventure, the boy I had a crush on, new things to explore.

A place where I could be myself.

But was that true? I mean, did I actually ever act like

myself around others? Did I really know how to act around others, or was it all just a lie? Was I simply trying to fit in all the time, or was this who I was? I felt as if I didn't know anymore, not after the condemning I received from my parents and the shadows I hide in at school. So the question really was, *who was I?*

"And if he's not to your fitting, I'll be here for you, Alice." Chase grabbed me and pulled me away from Malcolm. "I'm a better protector than that *Mad* Hatter over there."

Malcolm shot him a look. "In your dreams, *Cat*."

I chuckled at their arguing but decided to change the subject, as I could tell that it was only going to get worse. "So you guys have been looking for me for a while then. You have been at school for a month now."

"Yes. We had to make sure you were the right person. We can't just bring any human here," Malcolm answered.

I stopped and watched them carefully. "Why, what happens?"

"They don't accept the change and well…" Malcolm trailed off.

"Well, what?"

"They die," Chase answered as a matter of fact.

"Die?" I exclaimed.

Chase nodded and smiled as if it were some kind of game. "Yes, their bodies don't accept this world and they disappear, both from here and the real world. It's as if they never existed in the first place. No one remembers them except for those here. But in the real world, there is no one there to remember them, no one to mourn them. It's for the best, really, as no one in your world will know the truth. It's better that way."

I couldn't believe what I was hearing. How many people had disappeared? How many people hadn't accepted the change and simply ceased to exist? I had accidentally arrived at this place after getting pushed in the locker. Does that mean I could have died if I wasn't the one they were looking for?

"Speaking of which, how is your head?" Malcolm asked.

I placed my hand on my forehead. I had forgotten all about it. "Fine. There's no more pain."

"Good, you have nothing to worry about then." He smiled as if trying to reassure me.

It didn't work, I still worried that I would suddenly disappear, and everything would be gone. My existence would be no more.

But in the back of my mind, I wondered if that truly would be a bad thing. My family didn't like me. I only caused them trouble. I only had one true friend, and if I were gone, she was sure to have other friends, as she already had a lot more friends than I ever did. Would anyone really miss me if I was gone?

It was only a slight thought, a doubt really, and it passed as soon as it came. Even though my family disagreed with me, I knew they still loved me, and Kate was my best friend, and neither of us would have it any other way.

I turned to Chase. "You mean I could have died if I wasn't the correct person?"

"But you are, so you're fine." Chase placed his hand on my shoulder. "So don't worry about it. I wouldn't have brought you here if I didn't think you would be fine."

"But why did you erase my memories? Why didn't you just explain all this earlier?"

"Because we weren't ready. We still aren't ready, but the White Rabbit found you and made the first move."

"White Rabbit?" I tapped my chin with my finger. "Like the creature that Alice follows into Wonderland?"

"Yes, that little kid that tried to kill you was the White Rabbit," Chase explained. "So in a way, he brought you to Wonderland just like the original Alice."

The little kid. I had almost forgotten. "That little kid was the White Rabbit?"

"Yes, don't let appearances fool you. He's a dangerous person. He's the queen and king's right-hand man."

"Which brings me to another question. Why do you all look so young? I mean you look older than you say for school, but you can't be over twenty and that is pushing it."

Chase shrugged. "Age doesn't matter here. Most people are young here because the dreams that reside here are those of younger generations. Most of them disappear when they get to a certain age. Others stay, but it's rare. Most people let go of their dreams. They don't think they're as important when they're older."

"You mean people give up on their dreams? And therefore their existence here is gone."

"Yes, and they disappear into nothing. The problem now is that Morpheus is destroying dreams that haven't been forgotten yet, causing chaos on your side. People are becoming depressed, losing their vision, and even losing reality."

That made sense in a way. I felt like I was seeing fewer people my age really pursuing what they wanted. There was a sadness spreading through my generation. "And somehow I'm supposed to fix it all?"

He winked. "Something like that."

"And how in the world am I supposed to do that?" I asked because I didn't understand what I was doing there. And on top of that, I really believed I was still asleep. When was this dream going to end? It all felt so real though and was quite strange.

Once we approached the castle, Malcolm and Chase escorted me inside. I gasped at how grand it was on the inside, just as it was on the outside. Although the rooms were high and mighty, there wasn't much left in the way of decor. It seemed to me that it all had been raided. I didn't even know how long it had been since this kingdom was destroyed.

The castle was quiet, and I heard our footsteps echoing through the hallways. It felt like walking through an old church during the week when no one was there. Very eerie to say the least, especially since the only lighting came from the dirt-covered windows, making the room dim enough that it was nearly impossible to see what was in front of me. I grabbed Chase's hand, mostly because I couldn't see anything around and knew with his cat eyes that he could. I noticed that Malcolm glanced over at our hands but said nothing. I just hoped he thought nothing of it. I really just trusted that Chase could see, and this entire time he had been more open to me than the rest of them. God, I didn't know what to think.

We finally came to a room that had a fire roaring in it. It felt good against my skin as it was starting to grow dark outside, and a chill had swept through the land. As we entered, two people stood up from the couch with a smile on their faces.

"You made it!" Davis sprang up and ran toward us. He wrapped his arms around me. "I'm so glad you didn't get caught. I was so worried."

"Uh, thanks? Really it is thanks to Malcolm. He was able to get us into the clear," I said, not quite sure what to do as a boy was hugging me.

Chase grabbed him by the collar and pulled him away from me. "Get off her, you perv!"

"I'm not a perv. I was just happy to see her!" Davis yelled back.

"Yeah, yeah, like I haven't heard that one before. Give her some space, will ya? You think she wants some disgusting rodent touching her?"

Davis pushed Chase. "Stop calling me a rodent!"

Malcolm stepped up, which I was glad. I wanted to say something, but I didn't know them well enough to feel I could barge in on their conversation. "Knock it off, you two. Can you act civilized for once in your life?"

Chase appeared as if he was going to say something but didn't. His ears just turned down like when a cat was annoyed.

"Well, the time has come at last, I see," a voice said behind me.

I turned to find an older gentleman with graying blond hair. His blue eyes appeared to have seen so much through the years.

"Alice," the man said. "At last we finally meet. I'm Howard, or you may know me better as the Caterpillar."

CHAPTER X

I stood there in awe, not quite believing that the man in front of me was the wise Caterpillar from the stories. I mean, it wasn't that he looked stupid or anything. I just never imagined him being a scraggly man with worn-out clothes and graying scruff on his face. But by the way he held himself, I could tell he had an air of authority, and that was all I needed to believe him.

I bowed to him out of respect. It was strange to do as an American, yes, but after Japanese class and watching so much anime, it just became a habit that I had picked up. It was better to be formal than to not. "Pleased to meet you."

He laughed. "No need for such formalities. It's not like I'm a king or something. I'm just a man who has been around for a while and a tired one at that."

I straightened up. "So can you tell me what is going

on?"

He walked over toward the fire. "How much do you know, Miss Alice?"

"Not much. I just know there is a Dream Kingdom and the Cirque de Rêves is trying to destroy people's dreams in my world. That and I know that I'm involved somehow. That is about it."

"Good, good. I don't have to start from scratch. I'm glad my boys could give you that much."

"There is still a lot I don't quite understand. I was told that you would explain it all."

He nodded. "Yes, in due time. But first, Alice, I would like to know what you think of this world."

I blinked. "What I think?"

"Yes, of this world and of the people you have met so far." He laughed. "I guess that is hard when they're standing right there in front of you. Boys, how about you give us some time alone so we can discuss everything. Alice is probably getting hungry, so go fix up some dinner."

Malcolm nodded. "Yes, sir." And with that, he left with the rest of them to what I presumed would be the kitchen. Chase was the last to leave, as if unsure if he should leave me there alone.

"There, now you can say anything you would like. They will hear nothing from me." Howard grinned.

I always found it hard opening up to someone I didn't know even if they were supposed to be a professional. I had gone to a counselor when I was younger since my parents thought it was strange I was so introverted and quiet. They got nowhere with me because, honestly, I didn't want to change, and I never could talk to someone I didn't know that well.

I shrugged. "What am I supposed to say? This world is beyond my imagination. I'm flabbergasted at the thought of being in a children's book."

He chuckled. "Ah yes, Lewis Carroll's take on our little kingdom. He got some things wrong, of course. Whether that was Alice protecting us or if it was him not listening to her, I do not know."

"Yes, well, it is definitely a world that I never thought was possible to exist. And then I find out that there's some reason you all need me. It's a lot to take in."

He was silent for a moment, then turned to the crackling fire. "But there is something else, isn't there? That you want to talk about?"

I nodded. "I want to know if this is a dream. I want to know if this is just in my head or if it is real."

"So I'll ask again. What do you think?"

"I think I hit my head while closing a window and I'm lying on my floor in a pile of paint at home," I honestly replied. There was no point in lying.

Howard frowned, his attention not leaving the flower. "You really believe that? Or is that just how you're coping with it all?"

I didn't answer. Truthfully, I had never had a dream that seemed this real and lasted this long. I felt everything here, even the warmth of the fire on my skin.

"Besides," he went on, "even if it was a dream, would it matter? How do you know what is really a dream and what is reality? There once was a Chinese philosopher who had a dream he was a butterfly, and he was full of joy and happiness. Then he woke up and realized he wasn't a butterfly but a man. Yet in the dream, he had no recollection of being human, so he wondered, was he truly a man? Or was he now in the butterfly's dream? Reality is a lot more complicated than any of us understand."

A butterfly's dream? What was he trying to say? I stood there, watching as the fire crackled. A dream could seem real, I suppose, as in that story. But at the same time, how could I recall so many things in reality? Usually in dreams you forget reality and only dream.

So this wasn't a dream. This was real. Which meant Wonderland was real and that I was missing from the real world.

I covered my mouth. "This is real. I can't leave. I can't get home. How do I get home?"

Howard frowned. "You can't, Alice, not until the Cirque de Rêves is destroyed."

My eyes widened. It never occurred to me that there would be no way out of this. I just thought at any moment I would wake up and be home. Even though it wasn't a dream, it was definitely turning out to be a nightmare. "What? What do you mean I can't?"

"The portal between dimensions is being watched. If

you went home, you would be followed by the White Rabbit, and Chase might not be lucky in saving you again. The only way to stop it is to destroy the Cirque de Rêves, and then you will be safe."

I shook my head. "But why me? What does this have to do with me?

"Let's start at the beginning." He flicked his hand at the fire and the fire became alive. Figures appeared in the flames—figures of guards and a queen in red. The guards danced around the queen, and all those who were citizens seemed to be bowing in front of her. I watched in amazement, surprised that the fire could do such a thing.

"A long time ago, the Kingdom of Hearts ruled Wonderland," Howard explained as the flames flashed into a great kingdom. "People looked joyful as they went about their day, smiling and talking to other figures. We lived in peace and harmony. That is until the queen came."

The flames roared up and many of the figures disappeared. Chaos ruled over the transfigured scene. Guards had their swords out, attacking the once lively citizens. The queen stood up on a pedestal, laughing as they attacked her people, the people she was supposed to rule.

"She made everyone in Wonderland live in fear. This was supposed to be where people came to get away from everything but not when she came into power. She destroyed the link between worlds, and the dreams that once thrived here vanished. Everyone hated her, but we couldn't do anything."

The flame changed slowly and showed a girl in a dress following a rabbit down a hole.

"Then one day, a little girl came into our world by the name of Alice."

"Just like in the stories," I said.

He nodded. "Yes, just like in the stories. No one knows how the White Rabbit got to her or how she followed him, but she was able to go pass the barriers the Queen of Hearts put up."

The image of the White Rabbit appeared. He was the little boy who had tried to kill me, but this time he had bunny ears just like Melvin.

"That's the boy who tried to kill me."

"Yes, we're getting to that." The Caterpillar turned back to the flames. "Alice came and questioned everything. She helped understand that we didn't have to live in fear any longer. She and a group of us went against the queen and the battled lasted days…"

The fire sparked up, the image of men on horses with swords fighting, and there in the middle of it all was a little girl. She fought alongside them all even though she was still just a kid.

"And we won. We brought down the Kingdom of Hearts, and as fast as she came, Alice left us. She didn't even say goodbye but simply disappeared back into your world. But then something happened; the door was opened, and human dreams came back once again. We thought everything was perfect and that we would never have to worry about anything ever again. And never see Alice again."

Everything did seem perfect in the fire. People were appearing as a new kingdom emerged. It was the Red and White Kingdoms.

"But we were wrong. The Red and the White Kingdoms started to have grudges against each other, and fights broke out daily. The peace we knew for only a brief time was going away yet again."

"Is that where we are now? In the Red and White Kingdoms?" I asked.

Howard nodded. "Yes. They both wanted Wonderland for themselves and could never make a treaty. They destroyed many dreams in the process."

The flames danced around again, and suddenly Alice appeared. She was different this time. She was older, about my age.

"And then, as if by magic, Alice came back. She tried to put an end to the fighting but failed. Neither side would listen, and she gave up. Alice then destroyed the Red and White Kingdoms and vowed never to return to Wonderland."

He waved his hands over the fire. "That's when the Kingdom of Dreams came into existence. The king and queen have ruled prosperously since the fall of the Red and White Kingdoms. Then one day, a nightmarish circus came into the kingdom. No one suspected a thing. Everyone thought it was just a new district—a new place to venture to. But then dreadful things started happening—the dreams started becoming dark. Their faces clouded, and some had even disappeared. The king and queen found out, but it was too late. They were also shrouded in the darkness."

I shook my head. "But what does this have to do with me?"

He turned to face me. "I had a vision in this fire of a girl from the other side that could help us. A girl that also goes by Alice."

"That's not my real name. My name is Meredith. You have the wrong person."

He placed his hand on my shoulder and looked at me straight in the eyes. "The name isn't the important part. Besides, you survived the transition, which means you're meant to be here. You have a true heart, Alice, and that is the only way you can defeat this circus."

"A true heart? There is no way. I'm just a teenager trying to find her way through this world. I'm not the girl you're looking for."

"The fire wouldn't lie, Alice. You are the one who is supposed to be here. And it is up to you to accept that."

I brushed off his hand and walked to the window. "There must be some mistake. I'm not a fighter. I'm not someone who can do this. I'm just an artist. There is no way I can fulfill the same shoes as that Alice did."

"You are a girl with an artistic imagination. With imagination, you can do anything in this world. Don't forget that."

I shook my head. "But how am I supposed to defeat this power? I don't understand what is going on let alone how to defeat it."

"The original Alice left something in case she never returned. Something for her predecessor, which is you."

"What did she leave?"

He let out a sigh. "We aren't sure. She never said, and she hid it long ago. None of us have ever found it."

"Well, that makes sense," I whispered. I couldn't believe after all that, she would hide it and not tell anyone. How was I supposed to find it when I didn't even know this world? Everything was new. How would I know she left something for me?

"Just have faith, Alice. The answer will come to you and you alone. We will be here to help in any way you need us."

I felt a chilly wisp of air go through the room, as if the door opened. I glanced over, but it was still closed. I went back toward the fireplace.

"I also wanted to know what you thought of my boys," Howard said as he stepped up next to me.

I glanced up at him. "What about them?"

He shrugged. "Have they been nice? Protective? I know in the past that some of them have had some arguments with Alice. I just want to make sure history doesn't repeat itself."

I shook my head. "No, they have been very kind and generous to me. If they have any arguments, I would say it was with each other..." I realized I probably said too much.

Howard raised an eyebrow. "Oh?"

"I mean, Chase and Davis don't get along; they're like a cat and mouse. That isn't surprising. But it seems like Malcolm and Chase have some other conflict going on—something that goes deeper than their roles. I don't know what it is."

Howard sighed. "I had hoped they had gotten past their differences, but I guess not. Don't mind them. They just have had a bitter rivalry for a very long time. It won't change, apparently."

I looked back into the fire, watching it crackle and pop. "It's strange though. They seemed just like normal teens at school. I would never have guessed that they had a life like this. I would never have guessed Malcolm…" I blushed, realizing I had pointed him out of all the rest. It was probably obvious I had a crush on him. *God, I was so stupid.*

Howard chuckled. "Don't worry, your secret is safe with me."

I smiled, and at that moment, I felt a chill go through the air again. I glanced around, but there was still nothing that could have caused it.

"This is a lot to take in all at once though," I said. "I'm not sure if my mind even comprehends it."

"I understand. If you need some alone time, I have a room prepared for you. You can use it to freshen up for dinner. There are some clothes that the original Alice left that I kept. They should fit you. I'll have Chase show you the way. I have a feeling he is waiting for you outside."

I nodded and blushed at the thought of Chase worrying about me. "Yeah, that would be nice."

Just as he guessed, Chase was sitting cross-legged outside the door. Howard chuckled. "I see you're guarding her closely."

Chase quickly stood up. "Yeah, well, you ordered me to."

Howard nodded toward me. "Please show her to her room so she can freshen up before dinner."

Chase held out his hand. "Come on, Alice."

CHAPTER XI

Chase took me to my room where I was able to find some clothes that fit me. I pulled out a more medieval-looking blue dress, which was a lot simpler than all the Victorian-style dresses that filled the closet. Although they were beautiful, I didn't particularly want to put a layered outfit on when I was only going to dinner.

"That dress will look fantastic on you," Chase said as he apparently was still in my room. I thought he had left, as I had been so engrossed by the outfits.

I raised an eyebrow. "Pervert. Give me some privacy so I can change."

He held his hands out in defense. "Just wanted to make sure you found everything all right. I'll be right outside the door if you need me."

"Thanks," I said. "Seriously though. Thank you for everything."

He simply smiled as he closed the door behind him.

I quickly changed into the dress. It was a bit long, but that was fine. I glanced at myself in the mirror and sighed. My hair was messed up from not having a shower and having been on the run since waking up in the middle of the night. Short hair loved to act on its own accord. I was exhausted, and I couldn't wait for dinner and then be able to pass out on the bed.

My stomach started growling, and I decided I better head downstairs before my stomach hated me even more. I opened the door to find Chase still waiting for me.

His eyes widened. "Wow."

I shoved him. "Don't make fun of me. This was the fastest thing to put on."

"No, I meant wow, you look beautiful in that. Blue really suits you."

I blushed. "Shut up. Let's get downstairs to get something to eat."

I didn't particularly like receiving compliments on how I looked. It always made me blush, and I really hated blushing when there were a lot of guys around. I swore if I got another compliment, my entire face would turn red.

We entered the dining hall, which was ridiculously large compared to anything I had ever seen before. It was as big as a theater, with a table that stretched from one end to the other. It was like what you would see in a movie. I kept forgetting this was a castle and that a royal family used to live here. It kind of reminded me of *Black Butler* a little, and I wondered if a butler would appear and claim he was "one hell of a butler." Half of me hoped it would happen.

Malcolm greeted me at the doorway. "Lovely as ever. Follow me this way and sit next to me." He held out his hand.

I glanced over at Chase, who was frowning. I didn't know what to do, but Malcolm offered to seat me first. I grabbed his hand, and he led me to the table and sat me next to him and Howard, who sat at the head of the table. Chase ended up sitting across from me.

"I see you found some clothes. They suit you beautifully," Howard said.

I nodded. "Yes, I'll return Davis's clothes right away. Is there a washer and dryer I can use or something?"

He laughed. "No, we don't have such things here. Don't worry about it. Just leave them outside your door, and someone will take care of them."

"Oh, okay. Thanks." I wondered who would take care of it. Maybe there was a butler named Sebastian who hid away somewhere.

"Now." Howard raised his hand out to the food. "Let's eat!"

I didn't understand how, but there was an entire feast ready to eat. There was no way that Malcolm and the others made this. It had to have been magic, I swore. I mean, we were in Wonderland after all. I supposed anything was possible.

In front of me were sandwiches of all different types: cucumber, chicken salad, egg salad, and of course, tuna salad. Chase grabbed about ten tuna salad sandwiches. I laughed as he stuffed them in his mouth. It made sense now. He was a cat.

Along with sandwiches, there were many pasties, both savory and sweet. There were ham and cheese ones, potato and cheese pie, cottage pie, strawberry, peach. You name it, it was on the table. I smiled as I grabbed a shepherd's pie one and strawberry along with some egg salad sandwiches.

As for drinks, I should have guessed. There were at least seven pots of tea on the table. Malcolm had four glasses in front of him, each containing a different type of tea. He saw me staring at him.

"What is it?" Malcolm asked.

I shook my head. "Nothing. It's just that if I had any doubt of who you all were in the stories, I don't anymore."

Chase commented, his mouth full of tuna. "What's that supposed to mean?"

"There is a reason she portrayed you all a certain way in the stories," Howard said. "And none of you are helping your cases."

Chase swallowed his food. "Look, I have no problem being portrayed as a cat, but *Mad* Hatter here got it off easy. How the story portrays him is nothing like how he is in real life."

Malcolm's eyes darkened. "Watch what you're

saying. You know nothing."

Chase let out a laugh. "Yeah right. I saw you out there in the Dark Forest, and my eyes don't deceive me."

"Chase," Melvin said. "Shut up. Now. That was a long time ago. You know as well as I those times have changed."

"Right." Chase stood up. "Now he's as pure as the driven snow. I can't stand being around him anymore." He grabbed his plate of food. "I'll be eating on the roof if anyone needs me."

Howard said nothing as Chase stormed out and left us sitting there. I didn't know what to do or say. I wanted to go after him, but it sounded like he wanted to be alone. Davis had a worried look on his face as he glanced at Melvin.

"Good riddance," Malcolm said as he took a sip of his tea. "Now we don't have to deal with that feline."

The rest of dinner was rather silent, and I ate my food awkwardly, wondering if Chase would come back. He didn't.

Malcolm escorted me back to my room, and I thanked him for a delicious meal. He left me with a candle, as apparently old castles like this didn't have electricity, and I went into my room for the night, leaving out Davis's old clothes.

I found some clothes I could use as pajamas and changed into them. I sat on the bed and stared up at the ceiling. I was tired, but my mind was racing. My mind began to run through everything that had happened. My heart started to beat quickly as a panic attack formed. What if I couldn't leave this place? What if I got stuck here? My family and my friends wouldn't know what happened. They would be worried sick if I never came home. How much time had passed since I had left the real world? Would they know I was gone? Supposedly no time had passed for the real Alice, in the stories at least, but that was just a story. It could have been wrong; lots of time could have passed. Everyone would be so worried.

I sat up and rubbed my eyes. What was I doing? Why did I willingly go with these guys? Why were they so interested in me? What was I supposed to do?

There was so much going through my mind. I no longer could rely on any of them to keep me sane. I would have to find some other means to preoccupy my mind from unleashing all these anxious thoughts.

It wasn't fair. I had to be honest with myself—I was scared.

As I lay there in the dark silence, I realized I was thirsty. I should have gotten some water before I went to sleep. I sighed, realizing if I wanted some water, I should change back into the dress instead of the nightgown I found myself in.

Well, it couldn't be helped.

I got back up and quickly changed. It was dark out, but the windows let in some light from the moon. I opened the door a crack and glanced in the hallway.

There was no one around. I hoped I wasn't disobeying any rules by going out into the castle by myself, but I knew I would be quick, so it would be fine.

Heading down the stairs where I figured the kitchen would be, I moved past the room where I had met Howard. The door was ajar, and I could hear voices.

"Alice…" I heard someone say my name.

Curiosity got the better of me and I stepped closer to the room. Were they talking about me? And if they were, what were they saying?

"She doesn't understand what's going on, Howard. Morpheus will kill her," Melvin said.

"Give her time. She will come to understand how to beat Morpheus," Howard explained.

"Melvin is right. A lot is at stake. Are you sure she's the right girl?" Malcolm said. It kind of hurt that he said that as he was the one who seemed to have faith in me. Did he really not think I was the right Alice?

"Have faith. She's the correct Alice. Do you remember when the original Alice came? She was a little girl, and she took down the Kingdom of Hearts. This girl can do it. I have faith in her." Howard tried to calm them.

I took a deep breath. They were putting a lot of weight on my shoulders, and I wasn't sure if I could handle it. I wasn't the original Alice; I was just a girl from a small city who honestly had nothing going for her except always having a smile on her face. A smile that hid away the pain and worry of the future.

"We almost got caught in the forest on our way here. Bill followed us," Malcolm explained.

"They knew she was in Wonderland. The White Rabbit was in the real world and tried to kill her. They know about her and will retaliate," Chase added.

The room became silent. I held my breath as I listened closely.

"Then we will have to act fast. I would like you boys to go out to the Cirque de Rêves tomorrow. I want you to see if anything has changed there," Howard ordered.

"Yes, sir," the boys said.

I heard them move, and I hurried toward the doors to the balcony outside. I didn't want them to know I was listening in, and it was the closest place to hide.

The balcony stood above the once grand Red and White Kingdoms. It was beautiful to behold. The ruins that were left glittered in the moonlight. Trees that appeared to be maples, if maples existed in this place, danced in the wind, adding to the scenery. I couldn't help but stand there in awe.

I heard the door to the balcony open, and I cringed. Did they notice me listening? Or did they just see me outside?

"What are you still doing up? I thought you went to bed."

I turned to find Chase behind me. I smiled innocently. "I got thirsty and came down for some water."

"Ah, I see." Chase stepped up next to me at the

railing. "You weren't just coming downstairs to listen to our conversation?"

I froze. I didn't know what to say. I didn't make a habit of listening to other people's conversation, yet I kept finding myself listening into theirs.

"Don't worry, the others don't know. Only I could hear you." He pointed at his ears. "These always come in handy. Though Melvin should have heard too, but I swear he is as deaf as an old granny."

"I'm sorry, I didn't mean to…," I began.

He shook his head. "I don't care if you heard us. There isn't any information we should keep you from. We brought you here without explaining everything, hoping you can solve our problems. Nothing should be kept secret."

"You all don't think I can do it, huh?" I said.

"There is some worry, yes. But I trust you, Alice. I think you can do anything."

I shook my head. "No, the others are right, I don't understand what is going on. I'm not going to be able to go against this Morpheus. Hell, I don't even know what I'm supposed to do. Am I supposed to just fight him? Like with swords or fists? If that is the case, I'm way too weak and I have no idea how to even hold a sword."

"Well, we'll fix that. Starting tomorrow morning, we shall teach you everything you need to know. Hand-to-hand fighting, swords, knives, guns, you name it! We will teach it to you."

My eyes widened. "Really? That would be amazing!"

"But first you need to rest. You haven't slept for a while, and if you want to learn how to fight right, you need all your strength."

Sleep. That was a good one. In a place like this, after everything that had happened, I wasn't sure I could sleep ever again. "I tried that, but I couldn't fall asleep. There is just too much going on."

"You don't need to worry about things, Alice. Live in the moment." Chase pulled me toward the stairs. "Come, I'll take you somewhere you can get your mind off everything."

I looked back at the castle. "Uh… Are you sure the others won't mind?"

"Meh, who cares? They are all stuck-up anyway. It will be amazing, I promise." He looked at me with those sad, catlike eyes. "Please?"

I stared at him a bit longer, laughing. He reminded me of Puss in Boots in the movie *Shrek*. "Fine, where are we going?"

His ears perked up. "Come right this way!"

It was dark and the stars glittered in the sky with the moon. Moons actually. There were two. It was weird seeing different constellations and more than one moon in the sky. Chase led me farther into the White Kingdom's section of the area. There was no one around. It was really just the five of them living there. No other people from Wonderland were here any longer. I wondered how they could hide away in this place for such a long time.

A lot of the kingdom was covered in wilderness now, as moss and vines covering the buildings. Trees grew through the concrete, not letting man-made objects block the path of nature. We came to one of the larger trees, and Chase stopped.

"Hold on tight, Alice." He pulled me close and suddenly we were up on one of the higher branches.

I almost screamed.

"Don't worry, you're fine with me."

I glanced around to find a small tree house in front of me.

"Are heights a regular thing with you all?"

"Well, mostly me. I like heights, and if you're going to hang out with me, you're going to have to get used to it." He smiled brightly as he gestured around. "This is where I live."

To have called it a tree house might have been a bit much. It really was just a flat board. No walls, no ceiling. Just a floor and some padding.

"You sleep here?" I asked. It seemed strange to be sleeping outside instead of in the castle. But he was a cat, I supposed.

He nodded. "Yup! Cats like heights."

"And you thought this would help me relax? I don't like heights as you already know."

"No." He picked up a rock. "I brought you up here to see this." He threw the rock into the forest.

As the rock hit the forest floor, hundreds, if not thousands, of lights came shooting up into the surrounding sky. I watched them in awe. There were so many of them. They looked like fireflies, but something told me in my mind that they weren't. They flew more like butterflies. They spread across the sky, twinkling and changing color. I couldn't believe it. All I wanted to do now was paint what I had seen. As they rose in the sky, they looked like the northern lights, twinkling different colors. I could spend hours staring at them.

"This is amazing!" I exclaimed. "I've never seen something so beautiful."

"Wonderland is full of beauty and mystery. That's why I love it here. I always can find something new to explore." Chase sat down and leaned back on his arms. "I could never settle down in one place with so many things to explore."

I sat down next to him. "My world must seem so boring to you."

He laughed. "It's pretty dull, I have to admit." He glanced over to me. "But there are some great things about it."

I blushed as I looked back up at the sky. The lights still sparkled in the night sky. I leaned back on my arms and closed my eyes for a second. I didn't realize how tired I was, and before I knew it, I was out.

CHAPTER XII

I woke up to find a clear sky above me. I blinked a couple of times, wondering how that was possible. Then it hit me. I was in a tree. Way up in a tree actually. Chase had brought me up here last night so I could fall sleep.

That's right. I was in Wonderland.

So this isn't a dream. I'm trapped in Wonderland.

It hit me like a wall. I couldn't believe it. Deep down I had really thought it was a dream, but I should have woken up by now. I should have found myself covered in paint in my room. Instead, I was in a tree, by myself, with Chase nowhere to be seen.

Great.

I peered down at the ground. I had to have been at least five stories up. God, if Chase left me up there, I was going to punch him. I hated heights, especially ones where I knew there was no way I could get down without him transporting me. He was such a jerk if he left me.

After the anger dissipated, I realized how much I could see of the Kingdoms. Although I had walked through the ruins yesterday, it was much different seeing them in the day like this. I could see how grand it really once stood and how many people it could occupy. Most of the buildings now were destroyed by trees and plants, as I saw both white and red stones scattered around. The only building that was still standing was the White Castle.

There were also a lot of statues all around, representing different pieces on a chess piece. The red and white statues still stood with honor, showing that they were once a kingdom that ruled together.

I wondered what made them go to war with each other, especially since they were practically connected.

"Chase, where the hell did you go?" I whispered as I tried to figure out how to get down from there. Nope, there was no straightforward way of doing it. I was screwed.

"You didn't think I would really leave you here alone, now did ya?"

I looked up to find Chase on a branch a few feet above my head. I didn't know why I didn't think to look up.

"Who knows with you," I commented.

He grinned as he jumped down to the platform. "You

learn quickly."

I looked back down at the ground below. It seemed quiet, but I knew Malcolm and the others were there. "Shouldn't we be getting down there now? You said you all would teach me how to fight."

"As you wish." He wrapped his arms around me, and suddenly we were on the ground. He kept his arms around me, smiling. My heart started to beat faster. His skin was warm against mine, and I could feel his breath against my face. He started to lean in closer.

"Chase!" I heard Malcolm's voice call from behind me. Chase let go of me, and I turned to find Malcolm running over toward us. "You have some nerve, you stupid, stupid cat!"

Chase raised his eyebrow with a sly smile. "What are you talking about?"

"I went to wake up Alice, and she was gone. You didn't tell *any* of us where you took her. What do you think that was like? For all we knew, she could have been kidnapped. But lo and behold, you were missing as well." Malcolm had his hands clenched in fists, and his face was turning red. I stepped away from the two of them.

Chase shrugged it off, not letting Malcolm talk down at him. "She couldn't sleep, so I took her up to my tree fort to see the wonders of this land."

Malcolm looked up in disbelief. "You took her up there? How could you?"

"Easily. I'm a cat. Now stop yelling at me, or are you

just jealous that she spent the night with me instead of you?"

Malcolm pulled his fist back and punched Chase right in the jaw.

"Chase!" I exclaimed as he fell back. I knelt down next to him, making sure he was all right.

Chase placed his fingers over where his lip was bleeding. "That was uncalled for."

"No, it wasn't," Malcolm sharply replied. He held out his hand. "Now let's go, Alice. There's a lot we need to go over today. You don't want to spend your time with this cat."

I looked down at Chase, who was licking the blood off his finger. I didn't understand why Malcolm was so mad at Chase. He was just trying to help. Though, then again, he should have told someone where we were, but I was responsible for that as well. I sighed as I grabbed Malcolm's hand and he helped me up.

Malcolm led us back toward the castle where I could change into something more practical to learn how to fight in. I spotted an ivory-and-brown corset with a blue shirt, brown pants, and a utility belt that would be perfect to wear. I changed into it and met back up with Malcolm.

I glanced behind us to find Chase following at a distance, scowling. I felt bad for him and didn't know what to do. The more time I spent with either of them, the more they fought. I liked them both and wanted both to be my friends. I wondered if this was what

Tohru felt like in *Fruits Basket*.

"Why are you so mad at him?" I finally asked Malcolm. I would have whispered so Chase couldn't overhear, but I remembered he was a cat and could hear pretty much anything.

"Because he knew better than to take you away from the castle. If Bill attacked, he would have been defenseless. We have to stick together in case someone finds us," he explained, keeping his eyes forward.

"But would they have been able to get up there—on the tree, I mean. We were pretty high up."

"When Chase opens portals like that, they stay around for a while. Bill has a device that can allow him to go through. That's why we didn't use his abilities in the forest. If Bill figured out you were up there, you would have been cornered and everything that we worked hard to accomplish would have been for nothing."

I looked down at my feet. "Oh, I didn't know."

"You aren't the one at fault. Chase is. He should have known better."

"He was just trying to help me. I couldn't sleep last night. Too much going through my mind."

Malcolm looked over to me. "I know this is a lot to take in, Alice, but I think with our help, you can overcome anything." He nodded over to the other boys. "We'll train you in everything you need to know."

He led me to them, and they smiled when they saw me.

"Ready for a fun day of fighting, Alice?" Melvin smiled.

"If it will help me defeat Morpheus, then sure?" I had a feeling, though, it wouldn't help. I wasn't very athletic, but I was open to anything.

Melvin and Davis looked over at Chase and frowned. They didn't say a word, but I knew they were as mad at him as much as Malcolm was. Chase was silent as he approached.

We all at breakfast together. Chase simply lingered in the shadows, watching, making sure I was all right but not saying a word to any of the others, his ears down and a bit, ashamed. He acted like a cat who had gotten caught perching on the dining room table on Thanksgiving. It was sad to watch but almost a little comical.

Once breakfast was over, the four boys took me to an enormous room that was full of weapons. I gasped in amazement. It appeared like something that would be found in an English palace.

"To start off, we will work on hand-to-hand combat." Malcolm gestured for me to sit. "Melvin and I will demonstrate some fighting and then teach you a move, and you will try it with Davis."

"Why me?" Davis squeaked.

Malcolm smiled. "Because you're the smallest and best for her to practice with."

Melvin and Malcolm went out to the middle of the room. They bowed and then raised their hands. Right away I could tell that Melvin and Malcolm had two unique styles of fighting. Malcolm held his hands up but with fingers in, sort of like a tiger style that I had seen online, whereas Melvin had his fingers up and extended.

Melvin was the first to move. It all happened really fast, and I tried to keep up with how they were fighting, but it was rather difficult. When Melvin first struck, Malcolm blocked the attack with his left arm and then counterattacked with his right hand, slashing Melvin straight in the face. It was clear they weren't giving it their all, as Melvin recovered quickly. If it was full throttle, Melvin would have been on the ground.

Melvin swung his leg out toward Malcolm, bouncing back on his arm, knocking Malcolm's legs from underneath him. Although I would definitely have fallen face-first, Malcolm landed on his arms and tumbled back up to a standing position. The fight was clearly nowhere near over.

Malcolm took a punch at Melvin that was easily deflected, then Melvin punched Malcolm in the stomach. As Melvin was just about to hit him again, Malcolm grabbed his arm and pulled him toward himself, stepping out of the way and kicking him down to the ground. Malcolm knelt down as if he was going to punch Melvin in the face, but he stopped short.

"You get the idea, right?"

I nodded, eyes wide. They were good. I wondered how much better they were when they weren't holding back.

Malcolm motioned Davis and me to stand up. "Now you two come here. We'll show you the first move and how to deflect it."

I stood across from Davis, worried that whatever would happen wouldn't cause Davis any pain. He looked as worried as I did and as if he had been in this situation before.

"Now Davis, act as if you're punching straight at Alice's face, and do it slowly," Malcolm said as he stood behind me.

Davis's fist came slowly at my face.

"Now use your left arm to deflect it, and once it's deflected, use that momentum to punch him across the face. Don't actually do it but get the movement down in your muscle memory."

I nodded and did just that.

"Very good!" Malcolm said. "Now when he punches with his left hand, grab his wrist with your left hand and punch his elbow with the palm of your hand. Then with both hands, group his arm, pulling forward, and kick him in the knee."

"You suck as a teacher, you know that? She won't get anywhere with a teacher like you," Chase said as he still stood in the corner watching and ready to mock anything he could.

Malcolm turned and frown. "Really, you want to do this now?"

Chase shrugged. "Just telling you my observations.

You aren't that great of a fighter. I could beat you any day of the week."

"This again. You are just mad that I beat you last time."

"Oh yeah, how about a rematch?" Chase stepped forward. "And show Alice here what a real fight looks like, not this choreographed nonsense. You and me, one on one. No weapons, just fists."

Malcolm sighed, then motioned for us to move. "Fine, but don't complain to me when you have to crawl up a tree and lick your wounds."

I leaped out of the way, along with Davis and Melvin. Both of them frowned.

"Not this again," Melvin whispered. "What is he thinking?"

I didn't know which of the two he meant. Malcolm and Chase bowed and raised their hands. However, instead of a tiger technique or an open hand, Chase raised his hands like a boxer would.

"He's completely different from both of you," I commented.

Davis nodded. "Good eye. Neither of them ever agree on anything, even fighting techniques. That is where things get really interesting. Sorry you have to watch, but when Chase said no holding back, he wasn't joking. When these two have an excuse to physically fight, neither of them will stop until the other is down and out."

I stared at them, a bit afraid as to what would happen.

I didn't want either of them to get hurt. I knew how much they hated each other, and they used those matches to really lay into the other. I wondered how long I could watch.

Chase went straight toward Malcolm, keeping his elbows close to his ribs and punching at Malcolm's torso. Malcolm blocked them all and tried to rebut with his own technique, but Chase blocked him as well. Then Chase laid one right onto Malcolm's jaw.

I put my hands over my mouth as Malcolm wiped away the blood on his mouth. "Good one."

And with that, he punched Chase right into the jaw as well. Chase stumbled back for a moment, then charged at him with another punch. Malcolm easily deflected it and kicked him in the side. Chase blocked the second kick, adding a few more punches of his own. One landed straight into Malcolm's stomach, but he didn't let it faze him. Quickly he punched back, making Chase turn his back to him to block. Malcolm had the upper advantage for a moment, but Chase quickly got out of it.

"Oh my God, when are they going to stop?" I whispered more to myself than to Davis or Melvin. Neither of them were slowing down, and the more they fought, the angrier they appeared.

Chase took a large swing at Malcolm, which Malcolm easily dodged and kicked Chase straight in the face in retaliation. I watched as blood started to run down his face next to his eye. God, I couldn't stomach watching anymore, but my eyes couldn't look away for even a second.

Malcolm charged at him, round kicking twice at his face, but Chase dodged both of them and punched him in the face. Chase kept punching, but Malcolm held off each attack and punched him in the nose. He started to fall back, but Malcolm grabbed him and pulled him into a full nelson. Chase was helpless.

"When are you going to realize you can't beat me, cat?" Malcolm yelled. "Stop being a selfish bastard and realize you're nothing! Just a pain in my ass."

"Why should I ever take orders from you? You're an outcast! A criminal! You should have never been allowed back into Wonderland. Alice should have never accepted you. She was stupid to think you could ever change!" Chase kept struggling in Malcolm's grip but couldn't do anything about it. I wondered if they meant the original Alice—the Alice of legend.

"That is none of your business!"

"Boys, enough!" Howard stepped into the room. "Really, I leave you alone for ten minutes and I come back to this. How is Alice supposed to learn if you can't hold it together for a few minutes?"

Malcolm let go of Chase, and Chase dusted himself off. They both answered, "Sorry, sir."

"Chase." Howard sighed. "I want you to teach Alice how to use a sword. You are the best one to teach here."

He nodded. "Sure."

"Well then." Howard gestured to the swords. "Go

ahead."

Howard stared at Chase, scowling at him as he went to get the swords.

"Come on, Alice, we'll practice over here," Chase said. "There are many types of swords, as you can see. I'll give you a quick overview of what each is best at before we decide which one we should practice with.

"First off, you have your long swords and bastard swords, which are the typical medieval-looking swords. These can either be one or two hands, though with the heavier ones I think they need two hands. It really just depends on the handle. They are usually double-edged." He moved on to the next swords.

"For one-handed swords, we have broadswords, which include claymores. Then there are long knives, which are always good to have handy in case something happens to your main sword.

"Next we have the edgeless and thrusting swords, such as the xiphos, rapier, and panzerstecher, which are more for agility and finding your opponent's weak spot in their armor. Then there are the single-edged and curved swords, which include katanas, sabers, and cutlasses. Any questions?"

I had a lot of questions actually. I knew nothing about swords and suddenly was thrust into having to choose one of them. But there was one thing I wanted to know. "What would be the best to fight against Morpheus with?" I asked.

Chase scratched his chin. "Really depends on what

he has. It's not like I have seen him fight with a sword. As for the king and queen's guards, they fight with rapiers, which have more precision when dealing with armor. With Morpheus, you don't need to worry about that since he doesn't wear armor. You also won't be able to learn to be that precise and quick. As for double-sided, two-handed swords, I think they might be too heavy and slow you down. So really for you I would pick either a claymore or any of the single-edged swords."

I glanced back at the rest of the boys and Howard. They were all talking, and Malcolm seemed to be arguing about something, but Howard wouldn't have it. The tension was growing thick in the room.

Turning my attention back to the swords, I studied them all. I did agree that I would want to start out with something light at first, and there was one that stood out to me above all the rest. I grabbed the katana.

"I should have figured. All right." Chase grabbed two bamboo swords. "But to be safe, let's practice with the shinai instead."

I put away the katana. "That makes sense."

We went out into the middle of the room, and I pulled off the sheath and started to hold it by the handle.

Chase shook his head. "No, no, you can't hold your hands together or you won't be able to get enough power. Realize that the only part that really does the task of striking your victim is the last two inches, so you have to be able to torque it as much as possible.

You have one hand on the very top of the handle and at the end you have your other hand relaxed and controlling it."

He moved my hands to where he said they needed to be. It felt a lot more comfortable, and I started to understand how it affected my swinging.

"Great, that's it. Now block my shinai as I swing slowly."

He swung his shinai down slowly and I blocked it. He swung at the side, and I blocked it. It was fun, but I knew that this was never how a battle would play out with slow swings. A battle would be fast, but this was how I was to learn.

"Now move your feet with the sword. Keep a defensive pose. That's it!" Chase started swinging a little faster. "Great, but with a shinai and the katana, you block a little different. Here, like this." He motioned the sword at a downward angle. "That way it protects your whole body. Stepping back will also help."

I tried doing what he said and moved my feet with the shinai, but I kept messing up and left myself unbalanced. Chase struck again, and I lost my balance and fell backward.

Chase helped me up. "You have to keep your balance."

"I know. It's hard to think about all these things at once." I sighed.

Chase tapped his chin for a second. "Think of it like

this. It's a dance. A beautiful dance with sharp, pointy props. Let the rhythm flow through you smoothly. Just imagine the music is everything around you, and all that matters is getting the moves down and not letting your sword drop or the other sword touch you."

I thought about it for a moment. "All right. I'll try it that way."

Chase swung at me again and I recoiled. I didn't lose my balance this time. I let the rhythm of the shinai guide me. Chase struck again and again, and I blocked each one without a problem. He sped up his attack, and I kept up with him. Soon we were fighting at normal speed and the others just watched, surprised that Chase could teach me so fast.

Chase swung once more, but instead of blocking, I jumped to the side and knocked the sword out of his hand. He laughed.

"Perfect Alice! You got it!"

I smiled and curtsied as if I had just finished a dance. The boys clapped, and Howard looked very satisfied.

Chase turned to Malcolm. "She should probably go back to learn how to fight hand to hand. She's all yours now. Besides, I need to take a break."

With that, Chase left me there to train with the others.

CHAPTER XIII

After a couple of hours training, Malcolm let me take a lunch break. Howard had already made sandwiches and somehow knew my favorite sandwich: grilled cheese. The others finished their meals quickly and went back to the room to train. I took the rest of my grilled cheese and watched them.

To outsiders, they all probably looked like some kids just goofing off, but I knew better now. They were older than they appeared, a lot older, and training like they usually did. Malcolm used to serve under the Queen and King of Dreams. I couldn't believe it at first, but now that I watched him, I could see how he held his head in authority. He was a born leader, at least he appeared that way to me. The others respected him and followed what he said. Except for Chase.

Now that I knew them better, Chase didn't seem to

belong. He looked like an outsider, trying to fit in. I wondered what caused him to join this group to fight, especially when he hated Malcolm like he did. He was a loner and going from one place to another just like in the story. Did he just see Morpheus as a threat and decide to help the rest of them defeat him? But if that was the case, what had happened between Malcolm and Chase that made their feud so great? Was it so bad that they couldn't stop fighting for five seconds?

"Interesting lot of characters, huh?"

I turned to find Howard next to me. He leaned against the wall and looked out at them. Chase was still nowhere to be seen. I figured he must have gone back to his treehouse to be away from the rest of them.

I nodded. "Yeah, they are."

"They all have unique backgrounds, both good and bad. It's interesting that they're the only ones not affected by Morpheus. Then again, I can understand why. They conquered their fears long ago."

"Are they the only ones in this entire world who aren't affected?" I asked, wondering how it seemed such a small number. The odds of defeating Morpheus seemed greater than ever.

He nodded. "Yes."

I looked back over at them. "Why is that exactly?"

Howard shrugged. "It was probably because of all the things they have been through together. Chase doesn't let fear affect him since he spends his time alone and doesn't take things too seriously. Melvin has been through many wars and has already faced his fears more than once. Davis, even though he seems to be small and afraid, is strong-minded. And Malcolm…" He stopped midsentence.

"What about him?"

He sighed. "Malcolm has been through more than any of us can imagine. Morpheus can't make him afraid because he has so much darkness inside him already. It was said that the Queen of Hearts banished him to the Dark Forest. He used to be a troublemaker and is lucky to still have his head. He was all alone in that forest for years."

"What happened?" I asked, curious what their stories were, especially Malcolm. He was nice enough, that I could tell, but in his eyes it was apparent that there used to be some kind of darkness.

"Alice came, the original Alice, and she found him in those woods. She did or said something that persuaded him to come out of the forest and help her fight the queen. None of us could believe it; that boy never, ever listened to anyone. He was a lot like Chase in that he would only joke with people but on a much larger scale and was wanted for many, many crimes. But nevertheless, Alice spoke to him, and he listened. With his help, she was able to take down the queen. All seemed to be restored for Malcolm."

"But then Alice left, and he changed again. This time he was darker and colder than ever before. Whatever happened to the happy joker was lost in the Dark Forest forever. He became violent, and after a while and a few more crimes, he went back into exile in the forest. But as the story went, Alice came back. She found out what happened, and she went back for him even though we all thought he was a lost cause. It took a while, but he finally came to and tried to talk the Red and White Kingdoms into signing a peace treaty. It didn't work, and they ended up destroying each other."

"Then Alice left him again. They were very close at that point, but instead of going back into the forest, he stayed sane. So when the Kingdom of Dreams came, Melvin, who had served with him, recommended him to the king and queen, and he became their first general."

"So there are a lot of tragic secrets in Malcolm's past?"

He nodded. "Yes, and there is a lot that none of us know. We don't know what he was up to in the Dark Forest. You have to be very strong to survive as long as he did in that forest. But I haven't seen him this happy in a very long time. He trusts you, Alice, know that."

I shook my head. "No, they all have their doubts about me."

"I have a feeling after seeing you fight this morning, they have more faith in you. You did well, especially with that katana."

"Oh thanks. It was really Chase that did well. He explained everything in a way that I could understand." I turned to him. "Why does no one seem to trust Chase?"

He laughed. "No one really has trusted the Cheshire cat in the stories. I guess it has to do with him not having any loyalties through the wars. He leads people in all different directions, coming and going as he pleases."

"Why is he helping now? If he has no loyalties, I mean."

"This war is different. This war affects everyone and everything. No one is their self anymore, as they're becoming slaves to Morpheus. I guess Chase just couldn't stand not being able to play tricks on anyone any longer."

For some reason, I couldn't believe that was the only thing. Sure, Chase liked playing tricks on people, but there had to be more to it than that. There was so much more to him, at least that's what it seemed to me. "So that is why Malcolm doesn't trust him? Because he has no loyalty?"

"In the end, Malcolm trusts him to do what is right. They are the only ones left, and Chase can help them get in and out of places. He's the only one other than the White Rabbit who can travel to your world."

"Malcolm was pretty mad at him this morning," I said.

"Chase should have known better, but I know he was just trying to make you feel better. Malcolm will get over it. If he was truly mad, you would know."

"What do you mean?"

Howard smiled. "Let's just hope it won't come to

that. Now you should get back in there and practice. And don't mention this conversation to them. I don't think they would appreciate me talking about their pasts to you."

"Oh, I didn't mean to pry," I began.

He shook his head. "Don't worry, you should know who you're fighting with. That way you understand what is going on."

"What about you then? Why are you in the middle of all this?"

He laughed. "That's a long story for another time. Now get going; they're waiting for you."

I nodded, then turned to head down the balcony stairs. Now I was getting even curiouser and curiouser about it all, especially when it came to Malcolm and Chase.

CHAPTER XIV

We worked on fighting skills for the rest of the day. The sun began to set in the distance, and Malcolm called it a day. Dinner wasn't as extravagant as it had been the night before, but that was fine since I wanted to take a bath and clean up.

I was surprised and thankful to find that the castle did indeed have plumbing. I drew myself a bath and was able to soak in the warm water for an excellent amount of time. I was happy they had warm water as well. The castle was enormous, so I didn't have to worry about anyone waiting for this bath since they could go somewhere else. It felt fantastic on my muscles, as they were sore from fighting all day.

What I enjoyed most about the day was being able to learn how to use a katana. Chase was an excellent teacher, contrary to what Malcolm thought. I enjoyed being around Chase, as he could let loose and he made it his priority to let me know exactly what was happening, though I did think sometimes he could inform his own team more on what was going on.

I thought about Chase for a bit. He did finally show up at dinner, silent, still not talking to anyone, his ears twitching when others whispered about him. I felt bad, but I had no idea what to do about it. I didn't want to get in the middle of a feud that had lasted longer than I could imagine.

I sat in the bath for what felt like an hour, letting my mind wander. I had accepted the fact that I was now in Wonderland and needed to find a way out of here. If the White Rabbit and Chase were the only ones who could make portals, that would mean that I had to bring down the White Rabbit in order to go home, didn't it? That meant that no one could come after me once I went home.

No, I couldn't leave this place knowing what I knew —knowing that if I didn't stop Morpheus, then the entire world as I knew it would have their dreams destroyed and be living in a horrible mess. No, I couldn't allow that. I couldn't just turn my head and look away.

I never considered myself strong—far from it. But with everything going on, I felt as if I was growing and that I could do anything. I had learned to fight pretty well today, both by hand and with a katana. I still didn't understand why I was chosen, but at least now I believed I could put up some sort of fight.

And I didn't even have pink hair.

Getting out of the tub, I dried off my body and hair with a towel. Granted, it was a pretty old towel, but it seemed clean enough. As I tried to get the last of the water out of my hair, I heard a knock at the door to my room.

Quickly, afraid that whoever it was would barge in, I put on a robe and went to answer the door. It was Chase.

He blushed as he saw me in the robe. "Oh." He turned away. "I didn't mean to intrude."

I shook my head. "No, it's fine. Come in."

I moved over to the couch that occupied the front part of the room and sat down, making sure my legs were covered as much as they could be with the robe. He stayed standing, trying not to look at me.

"I just wanted to tell you we're leaving for the Cirque de Rêves tonight. The others didn't want to tell you, but I thought you should know in case something happens."

That made little sense to me. With everything that was going on, why wouldn't they just stay away from the circus until it was time to fight? "Why are you going?"

"To check their status. Morpheus knows you're here, and we need to figure out what their next move is." He scratched the back of his head. "No one believes you're ready to meet him, but I think you should see what you're facing."

"You think I should come?" I asked. I didn't particularly want to meet the man as he could control someone's fear. I had no idea what to do.

He shrugged. "If you feel you aren't ready, then no you shouldn't go. But it's really up to you. I just think you should have the option of going or not."

I looked down and fiddled with my hands. It was a lot to think about in such a short amount of time. I had just gotten here, learned all about the world, how to fight, but I was far from facing the truth of the matter and facing who I needed to defeat.

"You don't have to decide now; we aren't going to leave for another hour. I'll make the portal just outside the gate of the kingdom. If you're in time, you can still jump through it without me." He started for the door. "I should get back to the others before they know I'm here."

I quickly stood up. "Thank you for telling me all this. I really appreciate it."

He nodded and left me there. I stared at the closed door for a moment longer, then looked over to the clothes that lay on the ground from that day.

No, I shouldn't go. I wasn't ready. It would be a lot to handle, and I could fail miserably.

But I wanted to know what I was facing.

I quickly changed into some clothes and hurried out the door.

I headed toward where Chase said he would make the

portal. It was quiet out, as it usually was, but more eerie since I was alone. I hadn't truly been alone since I was here, and not outside. It was a strange thought to realize that in the real world I had been so used to being alone. Here, I wasn't even able to sit down long enough to gather my thoughts. I didn't know if I should be doing this, but Chase was right. I should see what I would have to face. Then maybe I could prepare.

As I came to the entrance to the kingdom, I saw four figures just beyond the gate. Quickly I hid and watched as Chase created the portal. Each of them stepped through it, and after they disappeared, I ran and jumped through it before it closed.

It felt like a jolt of electricity running through my body. It differed from the portal that led between worlds; it wasn't a feeling of falling. No, this felt a lot different, as if disobeying the laws of physics. It was over in an instant, but my heart kept racing. That was freaky.

I peered around at my new surroundings and gasped. Giant circus tents stood before me. I had never seen something so fantastic. The striped colors ranged from red to purple, swirling in a majestic rainbow. In addition, performers crowded outside the tents, juggling, dancing, eating fire, and even balancing knives. I couldn't believe my eyes.

Yet this is the evil causing all the darkness?

Crowds of people hurried toward the entrance of the tent. I noticed how they all had the same darkness clouding their face, just like the people I met earlier. Something here was indeed causing it, and even so, people still wanted to participate.

I caught a glimpse of Malcolm and the others ahead of me. Even though I knew they would be mad at me for coming, I knew it wouldn't be smart to separate from them. I just hoped they would forgive me.

As I hurried toward them, I notice that they had stopped in front of a man, and as soon I was close enough, I felt something strange. It was dark, almost like…

Fear.

Could he be Morpheus? I shuddered at the thought, but there was this lingering feeling in the air, the same one I got before an exam or before a performance. It was definitely the escalating feeling of fear.

The man was average height with a two-tailed suit and bow tie. The bow tie slowly changed color, and I was almost in awe with it. I really wanted one. He wore white gloves, and he held a black cane in his right hand. He also had on a black top hat covered in rainbow flowers that hid part of his brown hair. He looked like a ringmaster, and that's when I knew he had to be Morpheus.

"Well, well, it looks like you have a tagalong." Morpheus grinned as he saw me. Malcolm and the others turned around to find me standing behind them. I froze, wanting to run away. I should have stayed in the kingdom. This was a huge mistake. I wasn't ready for this; it was a really stupid idea.

"How did you get here?" Malcolm looked more afraid than I had ever seen anyone be. He looked as if he had lost all hope, as if I had done the worst thing imaginable.

Words escaped my mouth, and I couldn't answer him. I didn't know what to say. I realized I had just made the worse decision that could cost everyone everything. "I…"

"I told her we were coming here," Chase explained to him.

Malcolm scowled at him. "How dare you go against my orders." He looked as if he would hit him but held it back. I was glad though. I didn't want to see another fist fight break out.

Morpheus laughed. "Seems you have a bit of a problem on your hands, Mad Hatter."

"My name is Malcolm." His voice was dark, sending shivers down my spine.

"But you were far more interesting as the Mad Hatter. Oh well, if you don't want to take a trip into the past." He tapped his cane on the ground. "Maybe Alice would like to know."

Melvin and Davis stood in front of me.

"Oh, what do we have here? Two boys who think they can take on the God of Nightmares? How amusing."

"You aren't taking her, Morpheus," Malcolm said.

He grinned widely, as if this was a game. "Oh, but I

am! Haven't you learned anything? I always get what I want."

Malcolm pulled out his sword. It was a rapier, not a katana like I trained with. I felt against my side. My katana was awaiting my command. Was this the time to use it? Was I ready?

Malcolm pointed his sword at Morpheus. "You aren't taking her. Not this time."

"Oh ho! Brave little protector you are! Interesting given what you did to the last Alice."

Malcolm shook his head. "Your words won't distract me like they do others. Stop wasting your time."

He laughed as he pulled a sword out of his cane. It was also a rapier, dull on the sides and only pointed at the end. "Fine, I'll just kill you now and be done with this game!"

Morpheus leaped forward, and the clash of their rapiers rasped as they hit each other. Again and again Morpheus struck at Malcolm, but Malcolm was able to defend himself. Morpheus might have been fast in my eyes, but Malcolm was a lot quicker. The sound was loud as they thrashed back and forth. Morpheus tried to lunge at Malcolm, but it was no use. Malcolm was indeed skilled in fighting with a rapier.

Melvin, Davis, and Chase stayed by me, making sure I was protected in case Morpheus tried anything dirty. I wondered if I should pull out my katana and do something, but I felt as if I would be of no help. They were on a whole different level of expertise than me.

The others looked as if they wanted to stand up against him as well, but they stayed at my side, knowing Malcolm would be mad if they did otherwise.

A crowd gathered around, watching as the two swordsmen battled it out. Neither of them were holding anything back, and any second, one of them could strike a killing blow. It was like *Princess Bride* with Wesley and Inigo fighting on top of the cliff. I couldn't believe my eyes.

Then something happened. Malcolm lost his footing and Morpheus thrust his sword right into his shoulder. Malcolm fell back onto the ground, grabbing his wounded shoulder. Morpheus quickly stepped on his hand and kicked the sword away.

"Goodbye, dear Hatter. You will be missed." Morpheus pulled back his sword to give the killing thrust.

My heart was racing, and without thinking, I pulled out my katana and hurried to Malcolm. I pulled it up and blocked Morpheus's sword.

He let out a laugh. "Oh, Miss Alice, do you really think you can defeat me? With a katana, no less."

I shook my head. "No, I don't think I can defeat you, but I'm not going to let you hurt my friends." Taking a deep breath, I realized there was only one way to help them. "I'll go with you, but you have to promise not to hurt any of them."

Morpheus smiled. "Well, well, what do we have here? I guess you won the heart of this Alice as well,

Hatter. Some things never change." He looked over at Chase. "I bet some are jealous."

"Alice, don't." Malcolm shook his head. "My life isn't worth it. Just run away."

"She has already made her choice." Morpheus put his sword away and extended his hand out to me. "Now come, Alice. Wonder awaits."

I took his hand, fear engulfing me at his touch. He was powerful, that I could feel. I glanced back at the others, who just stared at me, knowing they couldn't do anything now that Morpheus had me in his hand. So I looked forward, realizing this was my choice, and I had to face the consequences.

But what those were, I still had no idea.

"You're a lot different from the Alice of legend, do you know that?" Morpheus said as he guided me through the crowd.

"I would hope so. A lot has changed in our world since then. Besides, I'm not that Alice. I'm an entirely different person."

He laughed. "I would suppose so. The old Alice was curious, sticking her nose into things she didn't need to. You, on the other hand, were dragged here without a choice, told to do this and that. You put on a brave face, but you know what? I can see the fear in your eyes. And they tell me you're screaming inside."

I tried not to listen to his words. "I could say the same about you. You are afraid of me. That is why you want me away from the others."

"Maybe at one point. I had heard whispers of your name and feared what you might bring. But now, seeing you as you are, I'm no longer afraid." He let out a laugh.

I felt a shiver go down my spine. I wanted to run. I wanted to run as far away as I could. He was right. I couldn't beat him. He really doesn't have anything to worry about. I tried not to seem afraid, but I knew he was aware of my fear. He was the master of nightmares, and I was exactly where he wanted me.

I shook my head. No, I wouldn't let him manipulate me with words like that. I knew he was just trying to make me scared, and I wouldn't let him win. I had Chase and the others behind me. If anything happened, they would save me, that much I knew.

We stopped in front of the main tent, and he turned to the crowd. "Come one, come all to the Cirque de Rêves! Don't let reality get you down. Let your fears grow all around! Leave happiness outside, and let the darkness come alive! So grab your friends, grab your children, and join us as we bring you on an adventure that will change your life!"

I couldn't believe it as people rushed toward the entrance. He talked of fears and death, and yet people came. The people wanted to be afraid.

The dreams wanted to be destroyed. How was that possible? What was he doing that was so enticing but at the same time destroyed them one by one?

"Come, I have a seat saved especially for you."

Grabbing my hand, he led me into the darkness.

CHAPTER XV

Thousands of people crowded the benches to see the wonders of the show. Each of them had darkness encompassing their faces. It seemed darker here, as if the shadows were growing over their entire head as well. Was this how it worked, black clouds slowly clouding their eyes and then taking over their bodies? And would I become one of them? Would I lose my dreams?

Morpheus led me to a seat in the front, smiling as if it was all a game to him, and it probably was. I didn't resist or try to run away, knowing there was no use. He was powerful enough to stop me. So I sat there, and I waited for what was to come. And more importantly, I tried to prepare my mind.

I looked back behind me to find Malcolm and the others sitting a few rows up. They looked worried, but they also knew they couldn't do anything inside this tent. I whispered that I was sorry. It was my fault all this happened. I should have thought it through. I wasn't ready to face him.

The lights above the audience turned off and everything became silent. I felt uncomfortable, as if chilled by the pure black color. I couldn't see anything, not even my hands in front of my face. I had always thought since I lived outside the city, that it was dark out, but at least then I had the stars and moon to guide me. This had nothing. I was trapped in a world I could not see.

And it was terrifying.

Never had I been so afraid as my heart pounded in my chest. My body didn't want to move for fear there was something out there. How was this a circus? How was this entertaining? And how did this lead to people losing their dreams?

"Alice." It was a whisper in my ear. "What are you doing here?"

I didn't recognize the voice. It wasn't Morpheus, but something about it seemed familiar. I didn't answer it but just tried to ignore it. I didn't know if it was my mind playing tricks on me or if there was someone calling me.

"Alice, are you listening to me? Shouldn't you be studying? Not wasting your time here." Whatever it was kept bothering me. Then I recognized the voice; it was my father's. Images swirled around me, and all of a sudden I was at home.

"Alice?" My father was now sitting across from me. He was mad; his eyes glared at me, and his face was redder than I had ever seen it. "You have been failing your classes! Why aren't you studying more?"

Report cards lay before me with *F*s all across the page. I shook my head. "This isn't real. I'm in Wonderland."

"What are you talking about? This isn't one of your stupid Japanese comics," my mother said. "How could you do this to us? How could you bring shame upon our family?"

I tried to say something but couldn't. I had no idea what was going on. There was no way that this was possible. It was all fake. It had to be.

Or was Wonderland fake and this was the truth? Had it all been just a dream? Was I back in reality?

I tried to remember how I could have gotten these scores. Did I forget to study for those tests? Was it finals? I kind of remembered finals coming up. Yeah, that's right, finals were last week. I was going to study, but I thought up some cool art subjects, and then there was the dance recital I had to prepare for. I didn't have time to study.

"Your sisters had perfect scores throughout school. Why can't you be more like them and not waste your time with trivial things like art and dance? That's it. I'm taking you out of dance until you can get your grades up. This isn't acceptable."

I shook my head. "No! You can't do that! I love dance!"

"You should have thought of that before failing." My father stood up and started for my room.

"Where are you going?" I called down the hallway.

"I'm getting rid of your art supplies. They are a distraction of what is really important. School."

"No! This is a dream! This isn't real!" I shouted, holding my head. *It had to be, right? This couldn't be possible.*

"Stop saying nonsense. This is real life, Alice. You cannot escape reality. You will never achieve anything at this rate," my mother yelled. "Why do you have to be such a problem for us?"

"No." I shook my head. "You aren't real! My parents wouldn't treat me like this. They know I care about my art."

"But you won't make it as an artist. You will fail and be all alone." The voice drifted through my mind. Colors changed around me, and now I was at my graduation. Kate was next to me.

"What are you doing here, Alice? Didn't you fail your finals? You can't graduate if you don't pass your classes. Didn't you get kicked out of school a few months back?" Kate asked.

"What are you talking about?" I said, tears falling down my face.

She looked at me in disgust. I had never seen her give me that look before. It was the same look that my parents gave me—the same one they gave me when I talked about my dreams.

"This can't be real," I whispered. "You're my best friend. You can't leave me. You are the only one who believes in me. If you leave me, I don't know what I'll do. I can't do this, Kate, please help me. Please tell me it will be all right like you always do. Tell me you're on my side."

"Get away from me, Alice. I don't want to be seen with a failure like you." With that, she walked off.

I shook my head. No, my best friend would never do that to me. She was always there for me, through being bullied, through each and every argument I had with my family. She would never leave my side.

"This isn't real!" I screamed out.

Colors shifted and I found myself on the street, all alone. No sounds, nothing. It was wet as if it had just rained. I looked up. It was pitch-black, no stars or moon in the sky. All the light around me came off a dying light bulb in the streetlamp.

"Hello?" There was no answer. "Is anyone there?" I started running and looking into shops. All of them were empty. No one was around. "Where is everybody?"

"Gone, Alice. You are all alone. No one wants to be with you." Morpheus appeared before me.

I shook my head, realizing what had happened. He was tricking me, making me see things that weren't there. "No, this isn't real! You are trying to trick me!"

He shrugged. "Doesn't matter. This is your future. There's no need to trick you. As you can see, you have so many horrible things coming that I don't even have to make any of them up. You will get nowhere, and people will leave you."

"That's not true! I have people who love me!" I screamed out. I was rocking back and forth on my feet. There was no way this could be my future—I had so much more to complete. Sure, I wasn't the best at school, but I was passing. There were plenty of art schools I could apply to; there were plenty of opportunities for me to succeed. I would never give up.

"That may be true now, but what if you fail? What if you don't get to where you want to go? Will people still be at your side? Think, Alice, will they still be there?"

More tears came flooding down my face. I didn't know what to think. He was right. If I couldn't get into those schools, if I started failing my classes, there was no way I could succeed. "I don't know!"

"To dream is to fail. You should know that. Why don't you think practically? Why don't you take the easy road? You were always trouble from the start, and now you have nothing to believe in."

"I have a lot to believe in," I whispered.

"Do you? Do you really?"

I tried to think of everything I believed in, but nothing but fear was in my mind. Fear of everyone I cared for leaving me. "Leave me alone! Get out of my head!"

He put his hand on my cheek. "Dear, dear Alice. If you wanted me gone, you would have already done so. You know I speak the truth, so you can't get me out of your mind. You are nothing like the Alice of legend. You are just a scared little girl who has no hope for a future. I can't believe anyone trusted you. You are not her. You will *never* be her."

I shook my head. "I'm not Alice. I never wanted to be Alice. I can never be as great. I can never defeat the Cirque de Rêves. I'm just a failure. The Alice before me was so much stronger. I have failed."

"That's right. You aren't worthy to carry the name of Alice. You are just an impostor, aren't you?"

I slowly nodded, his words penetrating like a knife. How could I be foolish enough to think I could fill her shoes? How could I be so foolish to think I could do the things she had done? I wasn't great. I barely was even living. I was just walking through life, not having a care. My parents were right. I was foolish.

Morpheus smiled. "But there is a way out—a way you can make all the pain go away." He wiped away my tears. "A way you can make all the trouble you caused others to simply disappear."

I looked up at him in hope. "There is?"

The surrounding image changed. I was at the coast now, standing at the edge of a cliff. Waves roared with the storm below me. I started to get dizzy, looking straight below as the wind whipped around me.

"Jump, Alice! End it all now!" I heard Morpheus call

out.

I stared at the ocean below me. "But there is so much to live for," I whispered.

"Is there? Think, Alice, you have lost everything. You have brought so much trouble to everyone around you. Your mother, your father, what do they need of you? They already have two perfect daughters. You are just a disgrace. Kate? Think of all the fun she could be having if she didn't have *you* as a best friend. She has so much potential. You're just holding her back. If you jump now, you can let them all be free."

It felt as the waves below were calling to me. They wanted me to jump; they wanted me to join them. They wanted me to be destroyed.

So I jumped.

CHAPTER XVI

A shock went through my body as I hit the water. I sank deeper and deeper, letting the water surround me. It felt warm and welcoming. I wanted to stay here forever. There were no worries here; there were no people here telling me what I could and could not do. Just the freedom to float and let my worries drift away. I could hide forever. I didn't feel as if I was suffocating. I didn't feel pain. I just felt nothing.

I could hear people calling my name in the distance, but their words were drowned out by the waves. I kept my eyes closed, ignoring whoever it was. I didn't want to hear what they had to say. I just wanted to be left alone.

"Alice, wake up," the voices called, but I ignored them. I didn't want to wake up ever again. I didn't want to go somewhere where my fears awaited me when I could just let the current take me wherever I wanted. I would no longer feel pain. I would no longer feel worry. I would just be free. I would just float here and not have to face anything again. It was all I could do; it was all that I was worth. Everyone had made that clear.

Whoever thought I was the same as the Alice of legend was wrong. I was clearly a failure and not capable of destroying the circus. I couldn't do anything to defeat Morpheus, and I realized that now. I couldn't succeed in anything I did, so I wanted to stay here and let my life pass me by. It was safe here; nothing to hurt me and nothing to make me afraid. It was peace. It was bliss.

Why didn't people do this more often? Just sit back and let life pass them by. It was soothing, refreshing even. There would be no more wars. There would be no more pain. We could all live in harmony if everyone just gave in to their fears and took the safe road. I could see that now. I had been a fool this whole time. This is what my parents wanted me to see, and now my eyes were open, and I could accept the fact. Dreams were worthless. They would never be achieved, not when reality would always get in the way, not when only pain awaited the dreams. Giving in to fear was the only way to go.

"Alice," I heard the voice call again. I saw a flicker of light, but I resisted it. I didn't want to leave this place. I didn't want to answer who was calling. "Please wake up."

I felt as if I was moving now, but I told myself it was just the current. I could see the storm above; the clouds were a bleak gray. That was the outside world up there, and I didn't want any part of it. I was finally free.

The ocean was a majestic blue. It went on for what seemed to be forever. There were no creatures, no people, just me. And I liked it that way.

Something tugged on me. Light flashed through the ocean. I shook my head and fought. "No! I don't want to leave!"

The force was too great. Whatever was trying to take me was succeeding. I felt like I was drowning. I couldn't breathe.

My eyes flashed open to find Malcolm's lips against mine. *Why was he kissing me?* I tried to jump back, but he gripped my head in place. I kept pushing him away, trying to get him to let go and let him know I was awake. Mouth-to-mouth was not supposed to keep going. Then I felt something weird, something in my chest, in my heart. It hurt, sharp pain piercing my heart. Malcolm didn't let go, his lips against mine. Whatever was in my chest felt as if it was coming to my throat.

Was Malcolm sucking? What the heck? What was going on?

He backed away, and I saw his eyes. They were black, solid black, like something off of *Supernatural*. If I had salt, I probably would have thrown it at him just in case. He closed his eyes and took a deep breath. When his eyes flickered open again, the black was gone.

I looked around to find myself back at the Red and White Kingdoms. Everyone was there, including Howard. Chase stared at me, and it was the first time I had ever seen him scared.

"What happened?" I asked as I tried to catch my breath. "How did I get here?"

"We brought you back," Chase explained. "I made a few portals. Hopefully they won't figure out which one is correct. They have a one in fifty chance of choosing the right one before they completely close."

I thought back to the last moments I remembered. I remembered going to the Cirque de Rêves, Morpheus taking me inside. Then the lights shut off. "That darkness…"

"Was Morpheus. He can control the shadows and make you see anything you fear," Howard explained. "He was successful in engulfing your mind into the darkness. Malcolm and the others brought you back here since you wouldn't wake up. They had to get you out of there; Morpheus had you in his clutches. You are lucky they got out of there when they did."

I placed my hand over my mouth and closed my eyes. I didn't want to remember that darkness. I didn't want to ever go back. Everything I worried about, everything that I feared could happen. I had jumped… I felt tears form in my eyes.

"It's all right, Alice. It's over now. You have nothing to worry about with us around." Malcolm placed his hand on my shoulder. "We won't let him get to you so easily again."

I shook my head and pushed away his hand. "I can't defeat him, not after what I've seen him do. There's no conceivable way."

Malcolm just stared down at me, not sure what he should say. I started shaking, afraid at what I had seen —at what I had done. Morpheus was powerful; there was no denying that fact. If he could control me, control what I was thinking, how could I defeat that? I had watched him fight Malcolm with a sword. Maybe if I had enough training I could last awhile using a sword, but there was so much more than that. He was more powerful than I ever imagined. He could get inside people's heads, and that was the end of that.

How was he even able to do that? How was he able to know what I feared—what anyone feared? Each being here was someone's dreams back in the real world. That meant that each and every person was dealing with the same darkness that I was facing. If that was the case, if Morpheus was able to get in each and every one of their minds, that meant he was in more places than one. *How could I defeat that? How could I get him to stop being in my mind and making me see things that weren't possible?* I just wanted to cry.

"Alice." Howard knelt down next to me and looked straight into my eyes. "You are brave. You can defeat him. You were able to go there and come back alive."

"Only because Malcolm, Chase, Melvin, and Davis

were there. Only because they pulled me out and got me to wake up. If I was there alone, I would be gone."

"But that's the thing. You aren't alone. You have friends who will help you. That is where you're stronger than Morpheus. He has no one but himself, and at the end of the day, that is what will win. You just have to figure out a way to defeat him for good. He's not that strong if you can overcome your fears. The real person you have to beat isn't Morpheus but your own thoughts. If you can do that, you can beat him."

"But why me? Why can't someone else defeat him with their mind? It already doesn't affect any of you. Why can't you all just go against him?"

"Because we aren't a dream. We aren't connected to any human. It makes it impossible for us to touch him. It has to be someone who has dreams; someone who can get past their fears and believe in something as pure as a dream."

"But what if I can't do that?" I asked as I wiped the tears away from my face. "What if he makes it so I never wake up again?"

"I'll always be there to wake you up, just remember that," Malcolm said.

Chase added, "All of us will be. You don't need to worry about that. Malcolm isn't the only one who can save you. You have us backing you up."

"How did you even wake me up?" I asked Malcolm.

"I took the darkness out of you and swallowed it," Malcolm explained as if it were that simple. I just stared at him. *Was that why his eyes were black? Because it really was like having a demon inside him?* It was crazy to think about, and if I wasn't in Wonderland, I don't think I could have believed it.

"But how?" I persisted. There were so many things that I didn't understand, things that I wanted to know about. I wondered if I could ever comprehend everything that was in this world. Probably not.

"Morpheus isn't the only one who has lived in darkness for most of his life. I'm not afraid of it and have learned to live with my demons," Malcolm explained.

I pondered what exactly he meant by that and what kind of demons could be lurking behind those light eyes of his. *Did I want to know?* Whatever it was caused Chase not to trust him. *What could he have done that made him seclude himself in the Dark Forest?*

"But what if you aren't there? What if I'm all alone? How will I wake up?" I asked. I knew I sounded pathetic, but after what I had just gone through, I knew I couldn't do it again by myself.

Malcolm grabbed my head and forced me to look at him. "You will never be alone, you hear me? I'll always be here to protect you. All of us."

I looked around and found the rest of the guys nodding. Even Chase was smiling, trying to reassure me that he would always be at my side, and for some reason, out of all of them, I knew I could trust him to be there the most. He never lied to me and always told me exactly what I needed to hear. I smiled.

"Thank you, all of you. I'm sorry I'm so weak."

"You aren't weak. Morpheus is just very strong," Malcolm added. "And knows how to find a person's weakness. All we need to do next is figure out what his weakness is."

Suddenly bells went off. They rang throughout the kingdom, echoing off all the buildings and statues. I jumped up, not sure what I needed to do. Was it a fire alarm or for an intruder? What did it mean? Everyone turned to the balcony, staring outside. No one was smiling anymore, and a stern look covered each and everyone's face. Howard pointed at me. "Stay with Alice. All of you. I'll go see what it is."

Quickly Howard ran outside and stared toward the entrance of the city. I had no idea what to do. Howard had looked scared, and that made me begin to worry all the more.

"What's going on?" I whispered.

Malcolm didn't respond to my question but kept looking toward where Howard had disappeared. "Melvin, Chase, watch Alice. Davis, you come with me."

Melvin and Chase nodded, and Davis hurried off with Malcolm to see what Howard was up to.

"Don't worry Alice, it's probably nothing. Sometimes these bells go off because of birds and such. Mosquitoes sometimes. Hell, even I have set it off a few times. Heh, that was fun, wasn't it, Melvin?" Chase smiled, trying to reassure me, but I knew better.

Melvin didn't seem to want to turn his attention back from the doorway. "Yeah, fun. You pulling tricks like that all the time is fun."

"Hey, what is that supposed to mean?" Chase seemed more bothered by the comment than the alarms sounding. He could keep his cool in almost any situation, it seemed. I envied that and realized it must have been the reason that Morpheus couldn't control him with fear. Chase knew how to put it in the back of his head, if he even felt fear. At the current moment, it didn't seem like he did.

"I mean," Melvin went on, frustrated as his cheeks were turning red. "This better not be one of your tricks, or I swear to God I'll kill you if Malcolm doesn't get to you first. Hell, if he did, I would just find a way to bring you back from the underworld and kill you again."

Wow. *Harsh.* I knew that Chase pulled some pranks, but he wouldn't even go that far to scare us like that. At least I hoped not. But it made me wonder what other pranks he had pulled to make them think he could be behind something like this.

"It's not," he whispered. "Not after everything…" He stopped talking, realizing he shouldn't bring it all up. Because we all knew, deep down, that there was only one reason those alarms would sound. Only one reason Howard would look so worried. Why Malcolm would leave my side.

Someone was here. Someone had found the base.

CHAPTER XVII

Melvin and Chase were silent as we waited for the others to come back. Although it was very likely that they had followed us to the Red and White Kingdoms, I still tried to believe that something benign had set off the alarm. I told myself to keep positive thoughts, but it was nearly impossible as I watched the concerned look on both Melvin's and Chase's face take shape. Even Chase was looking worried.

I wanted to lighten the mood by talking about something, anything really, but I was afraid to make a sound. They could be near us, and if that was the case, then we needed to be extra careful. I wouldn't screw this all up again, not that I hadn't already. It was my fault they had found us. I shouldn't have gone to the circus.

This was all my fault.

God, I was such a fool thinking I could be any match for Morpheus. He was stronger and better than me on so many levels. He could get inside my brain, and I had no idea how to get him out.

You are mine, Alice. You will never escape.

I blinked. Was that really him talking, or had that just been in my mind? Was it my fear letting him control me?

Does it matter?

I pushed back his voice. This wasn't the time to worry about such things. This wasn't the time to have self-doubt. I had to be strong right now. I had to stand up and fight with others if need be.

Howard, Malcolm, and Davis all came back into the castle, looking distraught. So an intruder had made it into the kingdom. We were under attack.

"We have to get away from this place." Howard grabbed a couple of swords and tossed them to Davis and Melvin. I patted my belt, making sure I still had my own katana at my side. "You two take care of her. Get her out of here. Chase, make portals to confuse them. Malcolm and I will hold them off."

Melvin put his arm around me and guided me toward the exit. "Let's go, Alice."

I shook my head. "No, I want to fight. I have to help you all. Please let me help."

Malcolm was the one to respond. "No, you aren't strong enough yet. We need to leave."

"But what if something happens to you? What if we

don't find each other again?" I asked, drawing my sword. "I can fight."

"We will find each other. We will all be okay. But in order for me to fight my best, I can't have you near the battle. I can't be worrying about you the entire time, okay? If you want to win, if you want to help, listen to me. Get the out of here."

I stared at him for a moment. He was right. I would be in the way. I would just be a liability. I put my katana away and nodded to Malcolm. "Fine. But promise me that all of you will be okay. Promise me you will come find us and we will defeat Morpheus together."

Malcolm put his hand on my shoulder. "I promise. Now run."

Turning to Melvin and Davis, I nodded as we made our way outside. The last thing I saw was the three of them talking to each other, figuring out their battle plan. I just hoped everything would be all right.

"Where are we going to meet with them? Was that even established?" I asked, realizing that no one had said anything. My heart started to race even more.

Davis nodded. "We know where to meet up, don't worry. It's our second hideout, about eight hours out from here. It's always been the meetup spot if we were ever attacked."

That made sense. It wasn't recently that they had to worry about getting caught. They probably had many backup plans to go off of. "Who is after us?"

"It's Bill, the man who chased us through the forest earlier," Davis explained. "He must have been at the Cirque de Rêves waiting for us. He's the only one who can reopen Chase's portals."

"And the White Rabbit?"

"No," Melvin answered. "He can only make portals to your world, not within this world. We figured making so many would take too long to sort out, but if we had known Bill was at the circus, we never would have gone. None of us thought he would be there."

"But that's better than Morpheus finding us, isn't it?" I questioned as we picked up our pace. While running, the kingdom seemed even larger, and I felt as if we were still nowhere near the boundaries.

Davis shrugged. "Really, that all depends on who you ask."

That was not something I wanted to hear, but I tried not to think about it. I tried not to think about getting captured and going back to that circus. I didn't want to face my fears all over again. I shuddered at the thought. No, I would not let him take control of me like that. I would not cower now and let him win. I focused on escaping and making it out fine. It was all I really could do.

We got to the edge of the castle courtyard and were finally in the city itself. I could hear men around us, yelling as they searched us out. We not only had to run, but we also had to be as silent as we could. Melvin grabbed my hand as we could hear a group of men get closer, and he pulled me around the corner into an alleyway.

At least I knew that the people I was with had the home field advantage, as this was a place they hid in and knew it like the back of their hands. The soldiers that attacked, however, probably haven't been in this kingdom for decades, if they even had been here. I wondered how many of them were dreams or if they had simply existed here forever like Malcolm and the others.

We didn't slow down for an instant. Melvin and Davis had a lot more stamina than I gave them credit for. I, on the other hand, did not. The only thing that was pushing me forward was adrenaline and the fact I didn't want to get caught. My legs ached like never before, even more than the one time I went to racquetball with my sister and her conditioning coach made us do drills for an hour.

More yelling surrounded us, and I wondered if they would find us and if all this running was for nothing. We had weapons, but would it really be enough? Would we be able to escape them if we came face-to-face? Maybe with the soldiers but with Bill I doubted it.

Although I understood how dreams could be clouded in the darkness, I wondered how exactly those who have always been in Wonderland could be affected. That had existed for so long, yet they still had fears. But of what? Melvin, Davis, Chase, and Malcolm hadn't been affected because they had learned to live with fear, but could it be possible they were the only ones who weren't affected? It was strange to think that people who have lived so long hadn't learned to live with their fears. Didn't growing up mean that you could overcome your fears? That was always how I looked at the world. I guess I was wrong.

We hurried farther and farther into the city, trying to get out into the woods where we could hide much easier, I presumed. I just hoped I wouldn't have to climb up any more trees, especially without Chase. At least with him, if I fell, he could easily catch me by making a portal.

I wished he were with me, as I felt most safe with him. Even though Bill could open portals, Chase could get us away from here and try to trick Bill into going somewhere else.

I hoped that they all were okay.

A couple of soldiers appeared before us, but Davis and Melvin pulled out their swords. Davis had a claymore while Melvin had a saber. It was strange that a lot of the people had different types of swords, but I guess it made sense after so many years they would all have their own preferences. The soldiers pulled out their rapiers.

Melvin was the first to attack. His saber slashed down toward the soldier. The soldier easily defended against it, but Melvin had only been faking him out. Quickly he turned the blade and swiped from the opposite side, cutting into the soldier's leg. The man fell to the ground, screaming out in pain, but I could tell he wasn't out of the fight.

The second soldier headed toward Melvin, stabbing his rapier straight at Melvin. Davis was the one who stepped in this time. He countered the attack with the claymore, which he held almost like a katana. Strength was found at the top of the handle and control near the bottom. It was starting to make more sense when I saw it in action.

The first soldier started to get up even with a wounded leg. Melvin slashed down at him, but the man deflected the attack and parried it.

I watched in amazement as those two men fought like they did. I didn't realize how good they were at sword fighting. It seemed like it was a necessity in this place.

Suddenly, as I watched them fight, someone grabbed me from behind. As I screamed, the person put a knife under my throat.

"Alice!" Melvin exclaimed as he cut down his opponent. "Let her go!"

Davis got distracted, and I watched as his sword was knocked out of his hand and the soldier punched him in the nose. Davis hit the ground.

Melvin started for him, but the guy who held me stopped him. "No, you stay there. I'm not kidding, or the girl gets it."

He stopped and stared at me, trying to figure out what we should do next. I struggled, but it was useless. Besides, this man had a knife under my chin.

That was it. A knife.

I still had the knife from earlier. I reached for it, acting as if I was still struggling as he kept his attention fixed on Melvin and Davis. The soldier was thrusting at Davis, trying to stab him through the stomach. Davis crawled away from him, attempting to get back in a better defensive position, but it was almost pointless. I had to act fast.

Drawing my knife, I stabbed the man who held me, straight in the stomach, moving my neck away from his own knife as I spun around and stabbed him again. As he went down, I pulled out my katana and deflected the other soldier's rapier as he thrust at Davis.

"Not today!" I yelled as I slashed forward, right through the man's torso. The man hit the ground just as the other two had fallen.

I just killed someone. He had been attacking my friends. There was no other way. But still… I didn't know what to think, but with everything going on, I didn't have time to waste.

Looking back up, I found Davis and Melvin just staring at me.

"What? Shouldn't we get going?" I asked, wanting to change the subject. I had to deal with this later.

"Yeah, let's go." Melvin put away his own saber. Davis quickly picked up his claymore and hurried after us.

As we ran, I noticed that it seemed like more and more men were following us. I hoped Malcolm and

Howard were all right after seeing many soldiers dashing through the city. *Were they only going after Bill? Or were they trying to fight them all?*

I heard the clashing of swords behind us. Malcolm and Howard must have been close. I felt a bit excited, knowing that they were still okay, but then I realized that meant Bill was near, and our chances of escape were growing smaller and smaller. I kept running, hoping that we could make it out of the city in time.

My legs were aching even more, the adrenaline starting to weaken. I was going to be so sore later, but if we made it out alive, I wouldn't care. The pain was nothing compared to what I had endured in the circus.

Just as we rounded a corner, Chase appeared in front of us.

"Chase—" I began, but he cut me off as he turned to Melvin and Davis. They appeared as if they were going to punch him.

"I'll meet you all there." With that, he grabbed my wrist, and the last thing I heard was Davis and Melvin yelling at him.

Before I could even blink, I was up high in the tree. It was the same place he took me the other night: his tree fort. I tried to catch my breath, but my heart was racing and everything around me was a dizzy mess. *Why would he pull me out of there? Had the plan changed? Had something gone wrong?*

"Calm down. You're safe here." Chase sat next to me, looking at the battle that was going on. There were so many soldiers I couldn't believe it. There had to be over a hundred running through the streets, searching for us.

"Why…?"

"They would have captured you if I hadn't intervened. They were naive to think they could just run away from Bill." Chase sighed as his attention was still on the city below. "This was the only way."

"I thought Bill could find portals. Won't he be able to find us?" I asked as I sat next to him. I might as well sit since there was no way down unless Chase took me.

Chase shook his head. "I made too many portals. He would have to know this was the right one."

I stared at the city. It was scary to imagine just moments ago I was in the middle of all that. "How did he find us?"

"I don't know. I made over four dozen portals. He shouldn't have been this prepared. If anything, he would have just sent scouts to each. He knew this was the correct one somehow," Chase said, frustrated that he had failed at his job. I felt bad for him, knowing that Howard and the others might blame him for Bill finding us. But I knew it wasn't his fault. There had to be something else going on.

"What now?"

He took a deep breath. "We wait. I told the others where to meet. We wait for everything to die down, then we will meet them there."

I looked back at everything going on, searching for

the others. I found Melvin and Davis running toward the edge of the city, knowing that they still had to act as if I was with them to keep the soldiers chasing after them. As for Malcolm and Howard, it took me a moment to find them, but when I did, I couldn't believe what I saw.

The two of them were fending off at least twenty men. *Were they really that strong? Could they really make it out of there alive?*

Malcolm promised me they would be okay; he promised me they would make it out safely and meet up with us. He had been there when we'd faced Morpheus again. But the odds were completely against him. There was no way that someone could fight that many men at once.

My eyes didn't leave the two of them. I couldn't see exactly how the fight was going, but I could tell that many of the soldiers had fallen to the ground from the two of them fighting at their full strength. Malcolm and Howard were back-to-back as they went up against their next attackers. Even though they were surrounded, they had the upper hand with that stance. I had faith in them, but the worry they'd lose still wouldn't leave my mind.

That was when it happened. The soldiers made them break their stance.

Chase slowly stood up, his cat eyes fixated on Malcolm and Howard. They no longer held a great defense since they were separated from each other. One of the soldiers thrust their sword at Howard, and I watched as the sword went through his stomach.

I tried to scream out, but Chase quickly placed his hand over my mouth. "Shh! They can't know we're up here."

After a few deep breaths, I nodded, and he let go of me.

"Alice, I have to go down there and save Malcolm. He won't be able to fight all of them by himself. I'm leaving you here alone. Don't make a sound, all right? You'll be safe. You just have to wait for me."

I wanted to say no, don't leave me, but he was right. He had to get Malcolm out of there. There was no way Malcolm could defeat all those men by himself.

Chase disappeared, and I peered down to see him appear next to Malcolm. Malcolm looked surprised and pissed, but Chase grabbed him, and they both disappeared to another place.

I looked around, searching for them, but I saw no trace. I closed my eyes and whispered to myself. "It's all right, Alice. He will be back. He will be back for you."

Minutes went by, which felt like hours, as my heart pounded in my chest. If anything happened to them, I would be stuck up here. *How would I get down?* I was at least five stories high in a tree.

I heard footsteps behind me. "Chase?" I spun around to find a tall man. It wasn't Chase. It was the man I had seen in the forest. It was Bill, his brown hair a bit messy as he had been fighting below. Blood stained his coat, but he didn't seem to be injured. He smiled as if victorious.

"Sorry, young lady, but your friends have failed to protect you. It's time you came with me." He started to reach out for me, but I quickly backed up and pulled out my katana.

"Get away from me!"

"Just lower your sword. I don't want to hurt you."

"Liar." I thrust forward, but he stepped out of the way of the attack.

"I see the boys tried to train you with a sword. How adorable."

I swung at him again and again, but he dodged each attack. He didn't even pull out his own sword.

"You better put that thing away before you hurt yourself," he said, teasing me.

"Stop treating me like a child!" I thrust forward again, but he simply stepped out of the way once more. This time though, I lost my footing and slipped backward toward the edge. Dropping my katana, I screamed as I began to fall down off the board toward the ground way below.

Bill caught my arm and pulled me back up. "Don't worry, I got you."

I looked down, imagining what could have happened. Pancake, that is what would have happened. "Why did you save me?"

"I told you, I'm not here to hurt you. I just want to

take you back to the king and queen. They have a few questions for you."

"Alice!"

I turned to find Chase standing there. He pulled out his sword to fight Bill.

"Sorry kitty-cat, but you lost this one." Bill kicked Chase straight in the stomach, and he tumbled off the branch.

"Chase!" I screamed as he fell toward the ground.

"He's all right. He can make portals, remember? Kitty-cat always lands on his feet." Bill pushed a few buttons on his wristband. "Now let's get out of here, shall we?"

CHAPTER XVIII

I saw none of the others as Bill took me by horseback toward the Dream Kingdom. I had to admit; it was awkward having his arms around me to grab the reins. I just hoped that we wouldn't have to ride this way too long.

There were still at least seventy soldiers left in the group, all of them surrounding Bill as he made his way back to the Dream Kingdom. I admit, I was quite relieved that he was taking me to the king and queen instead of to Morpheus. Although I knew nothing about them, I felt a bit safer not having to worry about going back to the circus—to the place that held my greatest fear.

I hoped that the others were safe and were trying to figure out a way to help me. Not that I only relied on them to save me, I would also try to figure out a way to escape, but I wanted to trust that my friends would help —that I wasn't alone in this. There was only so much I could do, and I didn't know everything about this place, but I would keep an eye out for any chance to run.

Getting rather bored with the ride, I started to look around me. Just as everyone else in the Garden District, each of the soldiers' eyes were masked with darkness. Morpheus had gotten to them as well. I wondered what all their fears were and why they couldn't overcome them. I also wondered why they were awake when I couldn't wake up until Malcolm took the shadow out of me. Maybe Morpheus did something different so I wouldn't come back. Maybe he did something that left me completely paralyzed. And, if that were the case, why did he go to such lengths for me? *Did he really think I was a threat deep down and didn't want to take any chances?*

At this point, it didn't matter. He was no longer worried about me being a threat, as he told me again and again. And, truthfully, I didn't see what I could do to bring him down and save this place. It was out of my reach to even consider doing something. On top of that, the supposed original Alice had left me something in case help was ever needed—in case her successor, which I still doubted was me, needed to fight. I wondered why she would hide something for another to find, but not tell a soul. *Did she not trust anyone here? Not even Malcolm or Chase?* That seemed hard to believe, but I guess if you didn't know what the future held, you couldn't be too careful.

How would I even know what she had left me? How was I supposed to understand something that was never explained? This place held so many questions, and it was getting annoying.

It hit me again. I had stabbed someone. In this place, all the citizens were dreams. Did that include soldiers? Or were they like in the stories of *Alice's Adventures in Wonderland* and simply here to fill a role? But either way, I couldn't have let my friends get hurt, no matter the cost. I owed them that much, as they had risked their lives for me.

Still, the idea left me shaking, and I didn't know what to think. I decided that I had to push those thoughts behind me and keep my mind occupied.

"Why don't you just transport me to the king and queen? Wouldn't that be easier than riding horseback the entire way?" I asked, sick of the quiet. Even with the enemy, I couldn't stand staying quiet for too long.

"Only the Cheshire cat can make portals. I just have a way to reopen them in a small time frame. That's how I found you. He wasn't very smart about putting you somewhere where you couldn't escape," Bill explained.

"He didn't think you would find the right portal." I tried defending him.

"Well, he was wrong then, wasn't he?"

I glanced around the wilderness that surrounded me. It was quiet other than the crunching of leaves under the horses' hooves. There wasn't another living being in sight.

"They will come for me," I stated as a matter of fact. "You will see."

"Oh, I'm counting on that. Otherwise this story wouldn't be very interesting." Bill lashed on the reins to make the horse start galloping faster.

It seemed like hours passed as we headed toward the edge of the forest and into the Dream Kingdom. Although I was practically being arrested, I kind of wanted to know what this kingdom looked like. It was called the Dream Kingdom, but did that mean the kingdom would be themed like the Red and White Kingdoms? And if so, what theme is a dream? Would it be all clouds, fluffy and serene? Or was it different and more of a hazy existence?

There still was no sign of the others. Although I knew Chase could pull through with his portal jumps and land safely on the ground below, I still hoped that he was okay. It was nerve-racking watching someone start to fall that high up. I had almost fallen as well, and unlike Chase, I couldn't land on my feet, so to speak.

I was lucky that Bill wanted me alive and lucky that he didn't just watch as I fell, my life ending right then and there. He needed me alive for some reason and had said that the king and queen wanted to see me. Why was that? Why would they want to meet me? It was confusing, to say the least, as all of them had been influenced by Morpheus. Could Morpheus be there as well? We weren't going to the Cirque de Rêves, but that didn't mean that he couldn't travel somewhere else.

I thought back on the last moments before Bill had captured me. Howard had died trying to make sure I got out of there alive. I couldn't believe he was dead. I couldn't believe all this had happened and I was still in the enemy's hands. That meant his death was for nothing.

Then it hit me. If I did escape, I had no idea where to look for the others. I had no idea where the meeting place was. Yes, they would probably be figuring out how to get me out of Bill's grasp, but what if I figured it out before then? What if I escaped? Then what did I do? It wasn't as if I could hide or ask for help. Another thing to think about on top of everything.

Once we came out of the woods, I could see the Kingdom of Dreams in the distance. I gasped. It was brilliant and more beautiful than I ever could have imagined. Everything around it appeared to be night, but the kingdom itself was lit like the starry sky. I didn't know if it was actually night or if it was always like that. It seemed to be daytime in the woods just a moment ago, so it had to be the natural state.

The kingdom was surrounded by small buildings, almost like an ancient-style Japanese village with paper doors and tiled roofs. Lanterns lined the streets, and everything seemed to be a dream, perfect to someone like me. If I hadn't just been kidnapped, I would have been pretty excited to visit such a place. It reminded me of a dreamier version of *Spirited Away*, which seemed very fitting.

When we got closer, I could make out more of the palace. It was a lot grander than anything around it. A large, steep bridge was the only way to enter the palace. It looked like something from the historic district of Kyoto or at least what I had seen in the picture. It glowed in the town like a gem in the rough. It was more colorful than I could have imagined, with royal purples, blues, and reds making up most of the walls.

As we entered the kingdom, I watched as people hid away in the buildings before we came close to them. They were afraid—afraid as everyone else was in this kingdom. Was it just a general fear, or did they fear Bill and his men? It probably had something to do with the Cirque de Rêves. Masked with darkness, they couldn't see the light. Some people didn't hide but went about their business. They didn't fear Bill like the others did.

Bill led the horse over the steep bridge. I looked down to see the palace surrounded by water. I could see orange glowing fish as they swam around. It was wondrous, almost as beautiful as Qinni's art, may she rest in peace.

We stopped in front of the entrance and Bill helped me off the horse. My legs were completely sore, but I still managed to walk like I was fine. Never show pain, that was my motto. That and I didn't know what they would do to me if I couldn't walk. I didn't say a word as he led me inside.

The inside was even more spectacular than the

outside. Everything was lit up, soft but bold, in solid primary colors. Lanterns hung from the ceiling, and I swore even the walls seemed to glow. Magnificent scrolls covered the walls that seemed to depict past battles. There was one that looked like the battle against the Heart Kingdom and one of the Red and White Kingdoms. They were beautiful, and I stared at them in awe. I wished I could paint like that.

Along with those gems, there were other paintings of various things such as butterflies, dragons, landscapes, and so on. Each one had to have taken hours and hours, but I supposed that they had a long while to create this decor, as the kingdom had been created shortly after the last Alice left over a hundred years ago.

There were many workers inside the palace, doing their daily job as normal, ignoring Bill and his men. They wore fantastic outfits, kimonos of all styles, and went about their business. I simply gawked at them, wondering if I could get my hands on one. But the realization that I wasn't here on vacation kicked in. I was here to be taken as a prisoner to the king and queen.

We walked farther into the palace, and more decorations and scrolls covered all the walls. I didn't say a word as Bill led me with only a couple of his men now following us. I wished I could read his face, but the darkness made it near impossible.

Bill stopped me in front of two grand doors. Dragons were carved into the wood, along with cherry blossoms.

"This is it, Alice. The moment you have been waiting for."

I held my breath as the doors began to open.

CHAPTER XIX

I couldn't believe my eyes. The room was magical, and if it weren't for being worried for my life, I might have enjoyed it. Glorious golds and reds swirled up the walls with more paper lanterns floating in the air above us. Steps led up to where the king and queen sat.

The king wore a traditional deep blue robe, the same color as night, with small stars that were sprinkled on it. If he stood in the window, I probably wouldn't have seen him. It appeared that he had brown hair, but it was hard to tell as his face was masked in the darkness. *Did that mean he would disappear as well?*

The queen, on the other hand, wore a light color, almost like that of a cloud. Light pinks, yellows, and purples accented the brightness of her kimono. She wore a light blue obi that made her seem more like a dream. As I entered, they stood up.

"At last we meet the spectacular Alice," the queen said as she stepped down the steps. "Was she a bother to capture, Bill?"

"No task is too hard for my queen." Bill bowed. I just stared at her. Her golden hair draped loosely on her shoulders. I wondered what beauty the darkness hid beneath. Her skin and hair seemed to be perfect, and she must have had such great beauty underneath.

She stopped in front of me. "What is it? Have you never met a queen before?"

"I have not," I answered, realizing that I had been staring. It was probably incredibly rude of me, and I felt stupid for doing such a thing.

"Well, now you have," she answered. "But what I want to know is why my dear Malcolm left my side and went after you. Why you are more important than his queen—the queen he swore loyalty to?"

I shook my head. "I don't know."

She let out a sharp laugh. "Such modesty, my dear girl, will get you *killed*. Now answer my question."

"I really don't know. They abducted me from the real world and brought me here. I'm still not sure why," I explained.

"Hm. The real world? Is this world not real?"

"I… I just meant my world."

"Both this world and that world go together; they cannot be separated. Each ties into the other," she snapped. "They are, in a sense, one and the same. Although I haven't seen your world, I would believe it is much like this one."

I glanced around. "Not quite, but sure."

The queen stood there for a moment as if examining me. "I still don't quite get it. My best men left me. Malcolm, Melvin, and Davis. All three of them left me for you. I don't understand why you're so special."

I shrugged. "I really don't know."

"And they were in the Red and White Kingdoms?" she asked.

He nodded. "Yes, ma'am. That's why her capture took so long."

"Not because Malcolm is a better soldier than you?"

Bill didn't answer, which made me start to wonder if what Malcolm had said earlier about him being better at tracking and fighting was true. I guess he had shown this entire kingdom how powerful he truly was.

But then I messed up, and here I was.

"I thought so," the queen added. "But Bill, do you have anything to say on the matter? Is this not the Alice of legend?"

"Your Majesty, this is the girl the boys had with them. Howard even gave his life for her. She's the one," Bill explained, trying not to upset the queen any further.

I felt my heart fall into my stomach at the mention of Howard. He had given his life to protect me only for me to get myself captured. I was such a nuisance. I should have learned how to fight better. I should have been able to protect myself.

"Then explain to me how this girl can be connected

to the Alice of legend." She pointed at me viciously. "This girl is feeble compared to her! She can't be the one they risk their lives for."

Bill didn't say a word as the queen approached me. Her face was right in front of mine, and I could almost make out her eyes. I think they might have been blue.

"What makes you so special? What makes you think you can overthrow this kingdom?" she yelled.

I wanted to back away, but there was nowhere to go. I was cornered with a queen yelling in my face. Not something I could ever prepare for, that was the truth. I was scared that she might order my head to be chopped off even though that was another queen's trademark.

"Answer me, Alice!" she demanded.

"I already told you I didn't know," I murmured. "It wasn't my choice to be here. Your White Rabbit tried to kill me."

She whipped around. "Where is that rabbit?"

"Right here, Your Majesty." The little white-haired boy appeared. I took a step back. He was as disturbing as the first moment I saw him. A little kid with rabbit ears yet more dangerous than anyone I knew, or at least anyone I knew in the real world. Everyone seemed to be dangerous in this world.

"Tell me why you think this girl is the Alice of legend," the queen demanded.

"Because she has the same mind as her. Just look at her eyes. She has that curiosity that always got the old Alice in trouble," the little boy answered as he stepped up to me, his face covered in a shadow now. Why he didn't have one before, I wasn't sure. Must have been because he was on Earth. "Yup, just like the old Alice."

The queen's lips pursed as she stared at me. "I suppose you would know since you brought the first Alice here." She clapped her hands together. "Then it is settled. You're the Alice we're looking for."

"I still don't think I'm…," I began.

"Shush, you're only to speak when spoken to!"

I shut my mouth quickly. I didn't see how this queen was any different in temperament than the Queen of Hearts, as Malcolm and Howard had said. Maybe the shadow was causing her to act like this.

"Now what are we to do with our dear Alice?" She started circling me, which made me very conscious of my body. What exactly was she looking for? "You seem so ordinary-looking. Although so was the other Alice, but the other Alice took down the Heart Kingdom and tried to stop the Red and White Kingdoms."

"Your Majesty," Bill said. "We did find the Cheshire cat with her. He seems to be helping Malcolm and the others."

"Well, well, isn't that strange? That little kitty never takes orders from anyone." She tapped her chin. "You must be one special girl to have that nuisance wrapped around your finger."

"He was with the others before I came along. It had nothing to do with me," I explained.

The queen laughed. "But everything has to do with

Alice. It always does." She spun around on her heel. "Take her to the dungeon. The boys will come for her, and we will be ready to capture them as well."

Bill bowed. "Yes, Your Majesty."

He grabbed my arm and led me out of the throne room.

And that was my first encounter with the Queen of Dreams.

CHAPTER XX

Bill led me down through the palace. I couldn't believe how many floors there were. Although it had looked large on the outside, it must have gone deeper into the ground because there was no way it could go on for this long down. We seemed to walk on forever. There were no elevators, which surprised me and made me realize that a lot of people here were pretty fit. It must have been due to having to run around all over the palace.

Once we got to the last floor, I noticed the smell of salty water beginning to sting my nostrils. It was so strong I could taste it. It reminded me of summers at my parents' beach house, if you can call the Oregon coast a beach. The water was always cold, and you always seemed to need a jacket even in the midst of summer.

We came to an area that appeared like a prison. I gulped as I smelled the stench of uncleanliness as many prisoners couldn't leave their cell. I wondered how long I would be down here.

I glanced around. I didn't see any way out except through the entrance we had gone through. There was only one way out, and it was heavily guarded.

Which meant escape would be very difficult in this place. Great.

Opening one of the doors, Bill shoved me inside. "Don't worry, Alice, soon your rescuers will come, and we will be waiting."

He laughed as he shut the door behind him. To say he was cocky was an understatement. Gathering myself, I peered around at my new surroundings. This room wasn't as brilliant as the others were, which made sense. This was the prison. The light was dim, all the walls were beige, and there weren't any beautiful lanterns to guide my way through the room.

There was a barred window on one wall, letting in a little light from the starry sky. I went over to it and peered out. Waves thrashed about just below it, letting in a mist of salt water. That was where the smell was coming from. There wasn't anything else under the palace except water, which also meant escaping that way would be near impossible. These people knew what they were doing.

"Wish they put in an actual window, eh? It would keep that cold water out," a voice said behind me.

I jumped, startled, and spun around to find a tall man standing behind me. He had a long trench coat on, and his fists jammed into his pockets. He peered out the window next to me.

"Glad they didn't take my coat away or I would be freezing down here in this cell." Turning back to me, he held out a hand. "Name's Kenny."

I slowly shook his hand, surprised I didn't notice another person in here with me earlier. Maybe I just assumed I was alone. Some of the areas were pretty shadowed. He must have been hiding. "Alice."

He opened his mouth wide. "So you're Alice. Glad to see the boys finally found ya."

"You know Malcolm and the others?" I asked, surprised that I had been thrown into a prison with someone else who knew the situation we were in. I wondered if all the other ones were full or if Bill had simply forgotten he was here. Either way, I was glad to have some company.

"Aye, they're friends of mine. I helped them out here and there." He gestured around. "Until I got caught. Which was just a matter of time, really. I'm very unlucky when it comes to getting captured..." He trailed off, as if he had many memories of being captured. I wondered how many times he had been locked away.

I examined him. He had quite a cute face, actually, kind of like a puppy dog. He was a bit older than me, probably about thirty. As for his eyes, they were large and brown. That's when it hit me. "Wait, your face isn't masked with a shadow."

He raised his eyebrow. "Just now noticed that? Brilliant, you are." He sat on the ground, cross-legged. He was quite a character indeed. "Now tell me, what did the idiot boys do to get you trapped down here? Why did they mess up protecting precious Alice?"

I turned, letting my eyes focus on the distant shore across the water. "It wasn't them; it was me. I screwed up."

"Ah, what did you do then? Had to be pretty bad to land you down here," he said, teasingly. I didn't appreciate his attitude, not in this situation at least. I had messed up badly, and he only saw it as fun. I could see why he found himself in prison more often than not.

"He captured us because I made the mistake of going to the circus," I answered. "It was… terrifying to say the least."

"The Cirque de Rêves. I know it very well." He rubbed the scruff on his chin. "Morpheus has definitely done a fantastic job being the God of Dreams, or I should say Nightmares. You have to at least give him credit there. None of us realized he was so powerful until it was too late. Hell, none of us even suspected a thing. I never should have let the king and queen…" He trailed off, staring at nothing. After a moment, he blinked, then smiled at me. "So I take it you didn't survive it too well either."

I shook my head. "No, I didn't." I looked down at the water and remembered jumping into it in my mind. The memory would always haunt me now every time I saw the ocean. "Malcolm had to take the shadow out of me."

Kenny nodded. "That boy eats darkness for breakfast; nothing can scare him. That's what makes him such a good warrior but also one scary-ass villain if he wanted to be."

"How do you know Malcolm?" I asked as I moved away from the window and sat across from him. I was done being reminded of that circus. I wanted to take my mind off it.

Kenny smiled. "Oh, me and Malcolm? We go way back, and I do mean way back." He started rocking back and forth as if excited to tell his tale. He acted like a little kid, but I figured he must be a lot older than that being in Wonderland. "I used to be a knave for the Queen of Hearts, you know, until I stole one of her tarts. Those damn tarts, she didn't eat them! She just let them sit there until they wasted away. It was a disgusting waste of great food. So I ate one and I liked it!"

"Just like the story then…" I was actually quite amused at how that still pissed him off, having happened so many years ago. I mean, did time still move the same here? If so, then it was over one hundred and fifty years ago.

He shrugged and scratched the back of his head. "I suppose so. I had a trial and everything. Malcolm was there. He lied for me; said I didn't do it. He was always a troublemaker even back then. Though more comical than anything. He just hated the injustice of the system and caused the queen a lot of trouble."

"He doesn't seem to be a troublemaker now."

Kenny laughed. "You wouldn't consider going against the Queen and King of Dreams, bringing you here, and trying to stop the circus troublemaking?"

He had a point. Although he wasn't as blatant as Chase, he had caused a lot of disruption in Wonderland. I really hadn't thought about it that way. No one here saw him as a hero. They all saw him as the enemy. "I guess when you put it that way."

"He is and always will be a troublemaker. Although he stood up for me, there were others who testified against me, and the queen found out Malcolm was lying. He had caused a lot of trouble, but there was never any evidence against him until then. So we were both sentenced to the Dark Forest for life, never to come out again. We shrugged it off, being two young guys who never imagined anything defeating us. So we were dropped in the middle of the forest in the darkness. The things we saw there…" His eyes became dark as if he were gone, lost in his memories for a moment. He came back and smiled. "Let's just say nothing can scare us after that experience."

"How long where you there for?"

He shrugged. "Who knows, really. Alice found us, tamed us in a sense, and brought us back. Or at least she tamed me." His voice became serious, which was strange after talking to him for a bit. I didn't think he could ever be serious. "Malcolm, on the other hand, was a different story." He slapped his knees, coming back to his cheery self. "But that is not my story to tell, now is it?"

I wondered what he could have meant by that. Malcolm seemed so nice, but everyone I talked to had known him in the past and said he had lived in darkness. What could that have entailed? I wanted to ask more questions about Malcolm and get to the answers of what people had been hinting at, but by the sound of it, Kenny wasn't going to give away any secrets.

"So how did you get thrown in this cell?" I asked.

"Oh, that's simple. I got caught doing stuff I wasn't supposed to. I spied on the White Rabbit and let Malcolm know what he was up to. I also did some research on trying to find you. Bill caught me. Good ol' Bill, he's always so persistent. Usually I like that about him; it's sexy. But this is completely different. Now he isn't his usual beautiful self. Have you seen his face? No, because it's shadowed in darkness. It's a shame, really. He has such a lovely face."

I wasn't quite sure what he meant by that, so I decided to focus on the beginning of his rambling. "So you're the one who found me?"

He grinned. "Yup, did all the research myself. I know your school, where you live, all those paintings you have."

"Umm… That is not something I wanted to know."

His eyes widened. "Sorry, that made me sound like I was a pervert. I'm not a pervert, I was just stalking you."

I shook my head. "That's… Never mind."

"I only did it so we could find the right Alice to help us save this kingdom. No other reason, believe me, I would never think of doing anything else."

"Well, you must have made a mistake. I'm not the Alice you're looking for."

He made an amused face. "Psh! I'm never wrong. You are *the* Alice; I should know since I've met the old Alice. You are her and always will be her."

I hated it when people kept saying I was the same Alice as before. She was legendary and much stronger than me, but then here I was trying to live up to her legacy. "But I'm a weakling. I'm not strong. There is no way I could battle like her or bring down any kingdoms whatsoever."

"You would be surprised what you're capable of. Just look inside yourself and you will find out."

I shook my head. "I already failed at that, I faced Morpheus and I lost."

"You survived though."

Barely, I thought. The only reason I survived was because the others pulled me out of there, willing to sacrifice everything. I would be gone if it weren't for them. "Because of Malcolm. I didn't want to wake up. I didn't want to leave the place he left me in."

"Well." His eyes became dark. "Then I guess

Morpheus has won and Wonderland is no more. Dreams that everyone has in the real world will cease to exist."

He made it sound like it was my decision—that only I could bring peace in Wonderland. That if I gave up, then everything would fail. "You can't place all that on my shoulders."

"Oh, but I can, because you're Alice and Alice shall save Wonderland like she always does."

I narrowed my eyes. "I don't like you."

He simply laughed. "That's what the old Alice used to say."

I had a feeling that it was what a lot of people said to him. However, even though he was a bit obnoxious, he was a pretty nice guy. I felt as if I could open up to him, which was strange for only knowing him for a few moments now. I have never felt like that before about anyone, at least not so fast.

A crash sounded from the other side of the door. Both Kenny and I jumped to our feet, not sure what was happening. Smoke came pouring from underneath the door, and I started coughing. The door swung open to reveal Malcolm. I stared at him, surprised that he had broken in so soon. I guess it was better than waiting for them to increase security.

"Well, why are you staring at me? Let's go!"

CHAPTER XXI

"Malcolm, my ol' buddy, my pal!" Kenny ran up to him and hugged him like a bear. Malcolm didn't return the hug but just stood there annoyed. "You came to rescue me at last!"

"I came for Alice, and you know that. We're in a hurry, so either stay here or join us in our escape." Malcolm grabbed my hand. "Let's go. We only have so much time."

Malcolm pulled me into the hallway and handed me a katana. "Here. Figured you lost your other one."

I took it and strapped it to my side. "Thanks." Although I didn't know how much help I could really do with it, as Bill had easily defeated me when I went up against him. Then again, he was one of the best soldiers in the kingdom, so I couldn't really compare myself to him.

"Ooh, I do love a good escape." Kenny ran in front of us, backward so he could face Malcolm and me. "What do we do next?"

"We escape," Malcolm answered as a matter of fact.

"Brilliant! Hey, did you get me a sword?"

"No, quite honestly I forgot you were even in here."

Kenny pouted. "Aw, how can you say that after all the things we've been through together?"

"Easily. I just simply put any thought of you in the back of my mind and let it disappear."

"Because your feelings for me are too great, so you had to let yourself forget. I understand now." Kenny smiled as if he had really believed for a second that was what Malcolm meant.

I turned to Malcolm. "He's strange, isn't he?"

Kenny laughed. "That's what the old Alice used to say as well."

Nodding to turn, Kenny led the way, running with his knees up way too high to be comfortable. I didn't even know how to take in the strangeness that was Kenny. It was like taking in every strange anime character I knew and combining them into some eccentric hybrid. Or maybe he was just like Vash the Stampede.

Alarms started ringing and echoing through the basement of the facility. We actually got quite farther than I thought we would before the alarm was sounded. I was surprised but a little worried. Something seemed off to me, but I couldn't quite figure out what it was.

As we made it farther down the corridors, Kenny

stopped and peered around as if looking for something.

"What is it?" Malcolm asked. He seemed actually concerned instead of ignoring him. So he did trust that Kenny knew his stuff. I probably would have ignored him if I were by myself. He seemed to have some weird quirks.

"Where is everyone? There used to be more guards down here," he whispered, his face now serious. How he could change his tune so easily, I had no idea. "There's a trap waiting for us."

Malcolm smiled. "I know. I planned on it. Bill thinks he can outsmart me, but as we all know, he can't."

Kenny laughed. "You always did think ahead. Nothing like me, are you?"

"Wouldn't be alive if I thought like you. How you managed not to be killed by now I have no idea." He started back down the hall. "Now we need to go this way."

Kenny and I followed Malcolm as he led us farther through the basement. I didn't understand why we didn't head up. Bill would catch us if we didn't start ascending soon, as that was the only exit to get out of this place. At least that was what I thought. I had no idea of how everything was even laid out. Malcolm must have had something planned.

"How did you get in here so easily?" I asked.

"It's always easier to sneak into a place than it is sneaking out," Malcolm explained. "Remember that. Besides, I used to live here, remember? I was once the king and queen's knight in shining armor, so to speak. I never cared for armor, always got in the way."

Kenny added, "That's for sure. A nice leather coat is always so much more practical. That is, until you're shot or stabbed."

"Which is why you just simply don't allow that to happen. You can wear all the armor in the world, but if you go against someone who is better at sword fighting than you, it will be all for nothing. A good offense is always a good defense in this world."

"And you try to say you aren't mad anymore, Malcolm. I think you lie."

Malcolm let out a quiet chuckle. "It's really just common sense. Something you lack by far."

"Who needs common sense when you could just be spontaneous?"

"Everyone. Everyone needs common sense. I have no idea why you don't understand that by now."

We rounded the corner to find four guards waiting for us. Malcolm pulled out his rapier in a single swoop and stabbed one of them in the stomach. As quickly as he could, he grabbed the fallen guard's rapier and threw it straight at Kenny's face. I seriously didn't think he was going to catch it and just end up with a sword through his face, but he did and joined the battle with Malcolm. I pulled out my own sword as one of the guards came at me. I tried to remember all that Chase had taught me. I blocked the few thrusts and slashed my opponent's torso. He fell to the ground along with Malcolm and

Kenny's opponent.

"Wow, Malcolm taught you well," Kenny commented.

"I didn't teach her," Malcolm said as he started down the hallway. "Let's keep going."

"Where are the others?" I asked as I ran beside him.

"It's easier for one person to sneak in than a group. That's something else you need to remember. Besides, it's better if they're on the outside in case we get captured again. Then they can rescue us. If they were here and we were all captured, who would rescue us then?"

"Excellent point."

We came upon a dead end with nowhere to go but back the way we came. The hall just simply ended. Malcolm stared at it for a couple of seconds and let his lips curl in a smile. It was all part of the plan. I just wished I knew what that was.

The sound of clapping came from behind us. Turning around, we found Bill and a dozen or so guards trapping us. If I could see Bill's face, I bet it would have been a look of pure satisfaction.

"Good show, Malcolm, good show. But where did you think you were going?" he asked.

"Tracked us the entire time?" Malcolm questioned.

"Of course. Who do you think I am? I just waited for you to make a very bad choice, which you did. Now you have nowhere to go."

Kenny stepped forward. "Oh, come on, Bill, what are

you going to do to us? You wouldn't hurt me now would you?"

"You're the first person I want to hurt, Kenny."

"So *naughty*, I swear. But you don't mean that, not after all the fun we've had together…" Kenny pouted. I really wished Bill didn't have his face covered in shadows so I could see his response. I felt like there was more to the story between those two, but knowing Kenny from these past few minutes, it was really hard to tell.

"Stop talking. You have nowhere to escape but back into our custody. There is no point in fighting, Malcolm. Just give up so your precious Alice doesn't get hurt."

I glanced at Malcolm, who was smiling, not afraid of Bill and the others.

"Are you so sure about that? That I have nowhere to go?" Malcolm asked.

Kenny examined Malcolm, as if trying to figure out what he was planning. Then a giant smile appeared on his face. "You, Malcolm, are brilliant! You are *brilliant*!"

Bill started for his rapier, but it was too late. Malcolm wrapped one of his arms around me and grabbed Kenny by his jacket with his other hand. Slamming his back into the wall behind us, the paper ripped and down we went toward the ocean.

I screamed, of course, because what else do you do when you're falling to your death? You scream bloody murder. Malcolm kept a firm grasp around me and onto Kenny's coat. Of course, Kenny laughed the entire time we fell. Malcolm simply closed his eyes, remaining calm as we were falling straight into the roaring ocean about to die. Then, suddenly, out of nowhere, Chase appeared, grabbing Malcolm, and away we went to another part of Wonderland.

CHAPTER XXII

It took a couple of moments to catch my breath. The air no longer tasted of salt but of wet moss and pine. We were in a forest now. Peering around, I saw the massive pines and oaks that shrouded the light from the sky. It almost appeared to be twilight out due to the tree coverage, but I had no idea what time it was. A light fog covered the ground all around us, which always did creep me out. I hated not being able to see the ground. You never knew what you were going to step on or what was going to grab you. Especially like that episode of *Stargate Atlantis*. I shuddered at the thought. There was a reason I didn't watch scary movies. First off, I lived by a forest. Second, I wanted to be able to sleep at night.

Kenny started clapping his hands. "Oh, that was fun! Can we do that again?"

Malcolm glared at him as he stood up and wiped off the leaves that clung to his clothes. He hadn't landed as softly as we had, which I had a feeling Chase might have done on purpose. "No."

"You can never have any fun, can you?" Kenny added.

"Not when you're around."

Kenny smiled. "You don't mean that."

Chase stayed seated on the ground, cross-legged, staring at Kenny. "What's he doing here?"

Malcolm finished straightening his tie. "He was locked up with Alice. I told him he could tag along if he wanted. Didn't actually think he would, but I figured if we ran into any trouble, I could just throw him at the enemy and save Alice."

Kenny laughed. "Such a joker, I love you, Malcolm."

"I wasn't joking."

"Well." Chase leaned his chin on his knuckle. "This changes things."

"But we're all about change now aren't we?" Kenny spun around, his arms wide open. "That's the beauty of Wonderl—" He stopped, face frowning. "Wait, I know this place."

Malcolm looked at him but didn't say a word. I tried to figure out what was happening, but I also didn't know what was going on. It wasn't like I could recognize places in Wonderland, except maybe the kingdoms from the stories.

"We are at the entrance to the Dark Forest," Kenny

whispered.

My heart skipped a beat. There was no way we would be going into the Dark Forest, was there? I mean, after everything everyone said, it sounded like it would be the worst place to go. *It had to be a joke, right?*

Chase stood up. "Brilliant, Einstein, you figured it out."

Kenny turned to him. "What's an Einstein?"

He put his hand on Kenny's shoulder. "It's an Earth thing, don't worry about it."

The sound of twigs and leaves crunching under running footsteps made us each turn to see what was coming. My heart raced in fear that Bill had followed us. Coming into view, Davis and Melvin appeared, looking beat.

Davis leaned on his knees, panting. "You landed a little off from where we planned. We could see you though, so we came over."

"Oh, I made you have to run. Sorry, pip-squeak." Chase smiled.

"That's not funny!" Davis frowned.

"It doesn't matter now, we're here." Melvin stopped the cat and mouse from arguing. "And now we have to start moving."

"What's your plan, Malcolm?" Kenny jumped side to side.

Davis looked at him in surprise. "Where did he come from?"

"Answer me, Malcolm, what's your plan?" Kenny

repeated. His seriousness was frightening me, especially since it didn't seem like he was the same person.

"We are going through the Dark Forest. You can join us if you want. Otherwise…" Malcolm pointed. "The exit is that way."

Turning, Malcolm began walking in the direction opposite to where he pointed. I glanced back at Kenny, who just stared at him, then followed along with the rest of the boys.

"This is suicide, and you know it!" Kenny called out.

Malcolm didn't even turn to look at him. "At least here I have the advantage. Out there, Bill can get her. Morpheus can get her. In here we can hide for a while and regroup without anyone bothering us."

"Other than the jabberwocky and everything else that is crawling through these woods!"

Malcolm was starting to get frustrated. I could see it in his eyes. He didn't like it when others questioned his authority. "Then come and help us fight them. You and I know these woods better than anyone else in Wonderland."

"What would Howard say about all this?" Kenny yelled after him.

"Howard's dead."

The words hit me like a wall. Although I saw it happen, although I *knew* it had happened, I had hoped that maybe, just maybe, some miracle came to pass, and he was alive. I wished what I saw wasn't real and that he was going to be waiting for us when we escaped.

Kenny ran over and stood in front of Malcolm, making him stop. "What did you say?"

"Howard's dead. Bill attacked the Red and White Kingdoms, and they killed him," Malcolm explained.

Kenny shook his head. "No, that can't be possible."

Malcolm shoved past him. "Well, it is."

"Then he finally woke up as a butterfly. His dream has come true." Kenny stood there for a long moment, staring at us as we walked into the woods.

I didn't particularly want to go, especially if Kenny, of all people, feared going inside. But what choice did I have? It wasn't like I could simply join Kenny without worrying about Morpheus finding us. Hell, this place had to be better than that circus. Nothing could be worse than one's own fears, right? As I thought about that, I heard a screeching sound come from deep within the forest. Maybe I was wrong. Maybe I agreed with Kenny and wanted to get the hell away from here.

As we kept walking, I could hear Kenny pacing back and forth, the leaves crunching under his shoes. At least, I hoped they were leaves, couldn't really tell with all the mist that seemed to swallow our feet whole.

All of a sudden Kenny appeared next to us. "Fine, I'll help, but don't say I didn't warn you."

Everyone became quiet as we pressed farther into the Dark Forest. I didn't realize that we hadn't quite entered the forest until now. It had already been so eerie that I couldn't believe it could get worse. It was like a haunted mansion except all outdoors. First off, there were cobwebs everywhere that were the size of yarn. I didn't want to see what those spiders looked like. Moss blanketed practically everything in the area, and trees, although thick and blocked out the sun, were practically leafless, and I swore some of them were glaring at me.

The ground was slippery and crunchy at the same time, and I really wished I could see where I was walking. I felt as if at any moment I could step into quicksand like in *Princess Bride*. This place was horrible and quiet now that we had gone deeper and deeper. I couldn't stand the silence.

"Have any of you heard of *Princess Bride*?" I asked. "I mean, I just really hope that there're no ROUS, you know, rodents of unusual size?"

Davis gave me the most horrified look I had ever seen. At first I had no idea why he was looking at me like that, then it hit me.

"Oh no, I didn't mean… Davis, I'm sorry…"

He put his head down as if ashamed he was a dormouse. I felt like such a jerk. He was a rodent in Wonderland and was probably picked on about it and I had just made matters worse. Chase simply laughed.

"Now that was funny, Alice! I didn't know you had it in you."

I really didn't. I wasn't even thinking about it when I said it. I decided to keep my mouth shut for a while and just hope that Davis would forgive me.

As we kept walking, the fog started to clear. I was

thankful that I finally could see the ground. This area was covered in grass, and flowers were spread out all around. It was quite gorgeous in a very creepy sort of way.

Out of nowhere, I started to hear voices, of children to be exact, singing. It echoed around me, bouncing off all the trees, making it so I couldn't figure out the direction it came from. I glanced at the others, wondering if they could hear it or if it was just in my head. None of them seemed to be bothered by it. I tried to ignore it, blaming my mind for making things up. But it kept persisting, the strange lullaby echoing through the forest. I could even see the tall grass and flowers sway to the rhythm.

"What's that singing?" I finally asked, persuaded that I couldn't be the only one hearing it.

"Ignore it, just ignore it. Don't let the words form in your mind," Malcolm warned. "Cover your ears if you need to, but it might not help. You just need to let your mind ignore it."

I nodded, trying my best to ignore the singing, but it was nearly impossible. With every step I took, it got louder and louder. Even when I covered my ears with my hands, I could still hear it. It was that persistent. My mind couldn't do it any longer, and before I knew it, the voices had gained formation in my head.

"Listen to our song, most majestic one. It's just a little tune to make anyone swoon. A lullaby just for you, help you sleep most precious Sue." Whatever it was sang in an innocent, childlike voice.

My body became tired and weak, as if my energy was being sucked dry. I couldn't think straight. Everything started to turn into a blur. How could I become so sleepy at a time like this? It made no sense. But the thought of a soft, comfy bed was to die for. All I wanted to do was curl up with a blanket next to the fire, snow falling gently outside as the smell of cocoa came from the kitchen. It was perfect, something I just wanted to dream about, and the more I thought about it, the more I convinced myself that if I fell asleep right now, I could enjoy it. I started to collapse on the ground when someone grabbed me.

"Up we go." Kenny pulled me up on his back to carry me. I didn't resist but simply rested my head on his shoulder. "Don't fall asleep. Never fall asleep with that disastrous tune in your head. Bloody flowers, such a nuisance to anyone and everyone. They don't care about anything except for their next meal."

My eyelids drooped, but I tried my hardest to fight it. In between my slow blinking, I saw them, flowers rocking back and forth. Daffodils, roses, tiger lilies. They were all singing—they were the ones trying to make us fall asleep. Why we didn't just bypass them, I didn't know. Maybe there was no way around them. My mind couldn't think in a straight line, but I knew I had to try my best to stay alert just in case.

The sound slowly died away as we moved farther and farther into the forest. My strength started to come back to me at last, and I felt strong enough to be able to walk. None of the others seemed to be fazed by the flowers, which made me feel a bit weak in contrast. I wasn't used to this place though. It wasn't like there was anything in the real world that I could have any practice with. I slapped Kenny on the side of the shoulder to let him know I was awake and ready to be let down. He set me on the ground.

"What the hell was that?" I asked as I stretched. Energy was slowly coming back, and it felt great.

"The Garden of Live Flowers," Malcolm answered.

"Which means what?"

"Which means," Chase said, "that they're living beings that feed off anything that they find. They get their victims to lie on the ground and fall asleep, then they wrap their roots around you and suck the life out of your body. Your blood becomes their juice and everything else their food in a sense. Most of them have been destroyed in Wonderland, except in the Dark Forest. No one wants to deal with the things here, so most people try to avoid the area. They must have been really hungry because they weren't trying to hide the fact that they were there."

They sounded grotesque. I couldn't imagine a plant doing such things. They were supposed to be such lovely things, not creatures that killed for food. Well, except for the Venus flytrap, but that was different. Well, it wasn't. It was just like that but at a bigger scale.

"Why didn't we just go around them?"

"Because there isn't a way around them. They are essentially the wall that keeps people out of the Dark Forest. They are just the beginning of all the horrible things this forest contains. They don't let anything in, but neither do they let anything out," Malcolm explained. "That is, unless you're used to their lullaby."

I didn't want to think of what worse things there could be in this forest. The more we strode farther into the forest, the more I wondered if the circus was indeed safer.

"So does that mean you all are used to the song? How is that?" I asked.

No one answered, but each of them glanced at Malcolm. Bill was the only who smiled. "Simple for me, really, I used to listen to their song for fun when I was exiled out here, hoping for a good night's sleep. Even uprooted one and planted it in my room, didn't I, Malcolm? Those were the good ol' days when we didn't have to worry about any rules or nothin'. But I guess it's better this way, having a sane mind and all."

"You are everything but sane, Knave," Chase commented. "And the Mad Hatter here has never lost his name."

Malcolm shot Chase a look, and before they began their never-ending argument, I decided to intervene. "How do we know Bill won't follow us?"

"Because this place is too dangerous even for him," Melvin explained.

"But what about the portal? Why didn't they just use

that?"

"It would have been very tricky for him to open a portal in midair where, if he messed up, he would crash into the ocean below. We actually planned it out instead of just going on a whim and getting captured." Malcolm eyed Chase. I had forgotten Chase was the one who had grabbed me and put me up in the tree where Bill had found me. I didn't blame Chase. There was no way Bill should have been able to find the right portal, yet somehow he did.

"It wasn't my fault," Chase argued.

Malcolm stopped and turned around to face Chase. "What do you mean it wasn't your fault? We had a plan, and you didn't stick to it!"

"If we stuck to the plan, we would have all been dead and Alice would have still been captured!" Chase retaliated.

Malcolm jabbed at Chase's collarbone. "If you didn't bring Alice to the circus in the first place, we wouldn't have needed a plan! Because of you and your big mouth, Howard is dead!"

Kenny held out his hand. "Malcolm, calm down. It isn't that bad. Just calm down."

"I would be calm if this cat didn't always screw things up for us."

Chase frowned, and the two boys glared at each other for a moment.

Chase shook his head and turned away from Malcolm. "Fine. I can tell that I'm not wanted. You don't need me anyway. This is your turf, not mine, *Mad Hatter*."

He turned and started into the forest, running away from the group. I watched in terror, as he would be all alone in the Dark Forest, a place where horrors simply awaited us all. I knew Chase was mad, but it was an idiotic reason to split from the group.

I glanced at Malcolm. "You can't let him just run off like that."

"I can't?" he sarcastically replied.

I shook my head. "No, because friends don't leave other friends behind." I started after him.

"No, Alice, wait!" Malcolm called after me, but it was too late. I was already out of sight from them as I headed after Chase.

CHAPTER XXIII

I regretted running off from Malcolm and the others, but Chase was a friend and I really believed that friends never turned their backs on one another. Even if he messed up, it wasn't a reason to completely kick him out of the group, especially when he was trying to do what he thought was right. Besides, they always tried to help me. It was my turn to return the favor.

I pushed through the scraggly branches, the sharp edges hooking on my clothes and ripping them. Blood-stained areas where my skin got caught as well, and I grimaced, hoping that none of them were poisonous. It was an afterthought, really, so from then on I made sure none dug into my skin. I kept going on, pushing myself farther and farther into the woods. There was no turning back now.

Especially since I didn't know the way I had come.

Even though I had run straight after him, I still didn't see any sign of Chase. There were no more singing plants, which I was thankful for, but the fog seemed to have grown thicker as I went on. Moisture formed on my hands, reminding me of a dark moonless night I had gotten lost in when I was younger. I heard the croaking of frogs around me but had no idea from what direction they came. The trees bounced every noise off of them, making everything seem to come from every which way.

Just like home.

I was glad Wonderland wasn't in a desert because I don't think I would have known how to handle that. No trees and only sun and sand forever. No, all those things were foreign to me, especially the sun. As it was already October, that wasn't something I was going to see for another five or six months. At least in the real world. Here, on the other hand, was a different story. The sun existed somewhere above me. I just had to get out of these woods, and I would see it.

At least, I hoped there was a way out.

Coming upon what appeared to be a clearing, I stepped out onto soft grass, praying it was indeed grass. It was mushy like grass, but since the mist covered everything on the ground, I really wasn't sure.

When I got to the clearing, I saw a rectangular figure covered in moss and blue star creeper. I looked up in the sky or where there should have been sky as foliage were thick. Curious what the rectangle was, I got closer until I realized it was a table or an object that used to be a table.

"What's a table doing way out here?" I mumbled under my breath. Even when I was alone, I couldn't stand silence and mumbled to myself. Yes, I was a freak, but I honestly accepted it.

I touched the moss, the fuzz tickling my fingers. In random spots, there were hard bumps underneath. I stuck my finger deeper into the moss, which in retrospect could have been bad, and pulled the item out from underneath the table. It was half a teacup.

I gasped. "This is…"

I dug for another item. A teapot. A spoon. A plate.

"The Mad Hatter's Tea Party. This is where the original Alice first met Malcolm."

I glanced around again. This wasn't the cheerful scene that was told in the story. No, this was dark and dank. Question was, had it always been this way? And if so, what exactly went on at these tea parties? I wouldn't think tea would be easy to come by way out here, especially if Malcolm never bothered to leave this place until Alice came around.

I set the items back on the table and laughed. I couldn't believe what I had found. If only Malcolm was here, then I could ask him more questions about what really happened, if he would even answer my questions. Thinking of Malcolm reminded me that I was lost, looking for Chase.

As I began to move back toward the forest, I felt

something brush up against my leg. Stopping, I looked down. I couldn't see anything. *Damn mist.*

I took a deep breath, trying to calm my beating heart. "It's all right, just a leaf or something. Nothing to be afraid of."

Then something went past my leg again. All of a sudden I was pulled onto the ground. All I could see was white.

"Come, walk into my parlor," a voice whispered into my ear. It didn't sound earthly but something of a screeching nature.

"Who are you? What are you?" I asked, trying to see if I could get a good look of whatever it was.

The creature stepped forward, closer, with its eight glowing red eyes staring at me. It was a spider. A frigging gigantic spider. "Will you come, will you?"

I shrieked as I scrambled to get back up. The worst scene in all of *The Lord of the Rings* and I was going to be living it. *Why was I so unlucky?*

"No, no, don't go, you must come and see. You must come into my parlor." One of its eight legs brought me back down.

"I don't want to see your parlor!" I yelled. "I want out of here!"

"Oh, but you must! You must! It's the nicest parlor you ever did see!"

"No!" I kicked and kicked, but I could not get loose from the spider's grasp. It spat out white webbing, encasing me in the yarn-like material that seemed stronger than steel. I struggled and tried to reach for my katana, but I couldn't move my arms. I was trapped. As it wrapped around and around me with sticky webbing, I screamed for help. Now I knew how Frodo felt, but for some reason, that wasn't a reassuring thought whatsoever.

"I have so many curious things to show you, my dear —" it began. Suddenly the creature let out a petrifying scream. It backed off me and screamed again. Firm arms helped me up. Once I was out of the fog, I could see my rescuer's face.

"Chase, thank God!"

He helped pull the webbing off me, slashing it with his knife. "What are you doing here?"

I took in a few deep breaths, still frightened about the spider. "I came looking for you."

"How could you be so stupid to separate from the others?" he exclaimed, serious fear in his eyes. Had he really been that worried about me?

I frowned, mad at the attitude he was giving me after I came to help him. "I could ask the same about you."

"But I have lived in these woods before. You have not. I know what to look out for." He pointed into the fog. "Like those spiders."

I shivered at the thought of that spider. "Thank you for saving me."

"I'm just glad you're all right, otherwise I probably would have been blamed." He sat up on the table. "Just like with everything else."

I sat next to him. "It's not your fault."

"Malcolm sure thinks so, and Davis and Melvin probably agree. I screwed up. I shouldn't have told you about us going to the circus."

I placed my hand on his back. "It's all right. You knew I had the right to know. It was my choice. I should have been smarter and not followed you. Or stronger and not let Morpheus get in my head."

He shook his head. "No, there was no way you were prepared for that. We should have known."

We were quiet for a moment, the croak of frogs echoing around us.

"How did you, well, you know, not let him into your mind?" I asked.

Chase looked up, as if he was staring at the sky except all there was were trees. "I'm not afraid of anything, I guess. I have always been alone, going from place to place. I guess he just had nothing to confront me on."

"You aren't afraid of being alone?"

He shook his head. "Not really. You get used to it after a while. It has been a long time since I had any real friends or anything. But it has taught me how to live for myself and do the things I want to do."

"Well, I know I couldn't be okay with being alone. I hate it actually. It feels like no one will be there to catch me when I fall."

"That is why you learn to land on your own feet. You can't only rely on others so much, and while it is great to have people around you to support you, it is up to you to make the final effort to stand tall. That is what I have learned and what I live by."

I stared at him for a moment, trying to take in what he said. I understood, in a way, where he was coming from. It was important to be able to stand up for oneself, but it was also important to surround yourself with those who will make you stronger. It was all about balance. "You're lucky not to have any fears."

He shrugged. "It's not that hard really. Just don't let anything bother you. Know what's supposed to happen is going to happen and just wish for the best."

"If only life were really that simple."

"You make life what you want it." He turned to face me. "And I know what I want."

There was a long pause where neither of us said a word. I finally turned away and looked down at my hands. It seemed like the only thing to do, especially since I could feel my cheeks starting to turn red.

"There you two are," a voice called at us. I looked up to find Malcolm and the others walking toward us. "I was beginning to worry."

Chase looked like he wanted to say something else to me but only stood back up and held out his hand to help me. I dusted the moss off my clothes.

"What is this place?" I asked Malcolm, hoping he would answer truthfully. I mean, it was obvious this was the infamous tea party from the books.

Malcolm stared at the table for a moment as if he

were somewhere else. After a few moments, he blinked. "Beats me."

I knew he was lying. I could see it in his eyes. I glanced over at Melvin and Kenny, who just stared at Malcolm. They knew the truth, but no one was going to spoil any secrets. It wasn't fair. I hated being left out of the conservation.

"Now let's go. We need to find somewhere we can stay before it gets dark." Malcolm started for the way he had come.

"This isn't dark?" I hurried to his side, glancing all around.

"If you think this is dark, just wait until night comes."

I looked up at the trees. I didn't want to know what kind of creatures would come out then.

CHAPTER XXIV

After what felt like an hour of walking, Malcolm stopped in front of a boulder that was at least the size of him, if not taller.

"Kenny and Melvin, give me a hand." Malcolm started pushing the boulder aside.

I couldn't believe they could move something so large. After their help, it started to budge, and I gasped. Was it just lighter than the ones in my world, or were they really that strong? As it moved, it revealed a dark cave. How the hell he knew it was there, I had no idea. He must have come across it before.

Malcolm looked inside for a moment, then nodded. "Yes, this is just how I left it. Doesn't look like anyone has been here since we lived here."

"We're going to stay in there?" Chase looked inside. "It's pitch-black. I mean, I can see everything fine, but the rest of you can't see a thing."

"Which is why we will find some trisings." Malcolm pulled out a vial from his pocket and tossed it to Davis. "Go find us some."

"Why do I have to do it?" Davis frowned as he examined the bottle.

"If you're so scared, then take the cat with you." Malcolm gestured with his hand. "Now go before it gets too dark."

"Fine." Davis started back into the woods. "Come on, cat."

Chase reluctantly left with him, rolling his eyes about the task.

"What do we do now?" Melvin asked Malcolm.

Malcolm sat down on a tree stump. "We wait for them."

"I know! Let's play a game!" Kenny clapped his hands. "Let's play twenty-questions. Okay, I'm thinking of a person, place, or thing."

"Alice," Malcolm said.

A look of disappointment appeared on Kenny's face. "That's not fair. How did you know?"

"You're a very predictable person, Kenny, just face it."

I laughed. I couldn't believe that he would pick me for the game, and the fact that Malcolm knew exactly what he would pick was even more amusing.

Kenny plopped down on the ground. "All right, mister hotshot, it's your turn."

Malcolm rubbed his chin for a moment. "Fine. I have one."

"Is it a person, place, or thing?" I asked, wanting to join in on the game. It was one of my favorite games to play on long car rides.

"Thing."

"Is it round?" Melvin asked.

"No."

"Is it large?" Kenny asked.

Malcolm thought for a moment. "Not large but not small. Moderate size."

"Can you take it with you?" Melvin asked.

"You could, but it wouldn't be practical."

"Is there one in these woods?" I asked. I still had no idea what it could be at that point, but I was trying to eliminate anything around us.

"Theoretically there could be one in *these* woods, but usually they aren't found in a forest if that is what you're asking."

Kenny scratched the scruff on his chin. "Is it heavy?"

"It can be, or it can be light."

"Is it something that can be found in both the real world and Wonderland?" I asked. This was getting intense and a lot of fun. I was glad we had something to take our mind off everything.

"Good question. It can be found in both."

"Does it have practical use?" Melvin asked.

"Yes."

"Do people use it on a daily basis?" I asked.

"Mostly, yes."

"Oh, oh! I know." Kenny jumped up and down. "Is it a toilet?"

I hit my head with my palm. Did he really think that Malcolm would pick that? He had so much more class than that.

"No."

"Damn," Kenny whispered.

"Do you sit on it?" I asked.

"Its purpose isn't to be sat on," he answered. He was particular with his answer. That meant we were getting closer.

"Is it flat?" Melvin asked.

Malcolm nodded. "Yes.

"Is it a table?" Melvin asked.

"Not quite."

"Oh, oh!" Kenny shouted.

"Is it a desk?" I asked.

Malcolm smiled. "Yes. Good job."

"Hey, I was going to say that." Kenny frowned.

I stuck my tongue out at him and laughed.

"It's your turn, Alice," Malcolm said.

I thought for a moment, then smiled. "All right, I got it!"

"Person, place, or thing?" Melvin asked.

"Thing," I answered.

"A paintbrush," Malcolm said.

I frowned. I hadn't even thought of it until they asked me what I should pick. How in the world could he have known that? It also was no fun when someone could always guess what the other person was thinking, as he had done this to Kenny as well. "How did you know?"

Malcolm laughed. "You all are so predictable."

"Found them!" Davis appeared with Chase at his side, his arms still crossed, not happy that he was sent on a task with Davis. Davis held up a jar, looking a bit scratched up. I wondered what had happened for him to look like that.

"Have any trouble?" Malcolm took the jar from him.

Davis gave him a look. "Seriously? You're going to ask me that?"

Malcolm chuckled as he took the jar into the cave. All of a sudden, the jar began to light up. I gasped. Inside the jar were little figures. They looked like people almost—like fairies.

"Fairies," I whispered. I couldn't believe what I was seeing. Did they actually exist?

"They are called trisings," Kenny explained as he examined them closely and tapped the glass. The trisings jumped back from where his finger hit the glass. "Sort of like a fairy but smaller and they only come out at night. More like fireflies but can last through the entire night. Really hard to catch."

"What is Malcolm using them for?" I asked.

"To light up the cave, of course. It's not safe to be anywhere in this forest without some kind of light."

"Oh." I forgot that it was supposed to be getting dark soon, as the woods itself seemed dark already. I just hoped the light coming off these creatures would be enough.

"The creatures that come out at night are far worse than anything in the day," Malcolm said as he had overheard our conversation. "So you never want to be without light. It scares them off." He sat the jar down and looked at the beings inside. "I just need you for a night. In the morning, I'll let you go."

The creature pounded its tiny fists against the glass, mouth moving as if it were yelling obscenities. I couldn't hear anything though. Either they were too quiet, or the jar had interfered.

Malcolm stood up and turned to the rest of us. "We will take turns keeping watch. I'll take first round. Everyone else, get as much rest as you can. You'll need it."

I peered around to find only rock around me. Since Malcolm acted like he used to stay here when he lived in the forest, I figured it would have a little more to it. I was wrong. It was just like any other cave one would find. I sighed, knowing that there was no way I would be able to sleep tonight. What did one have to do to get some good sleep in Wonderland?

Oh, that's right, destroy the circus.

CHAPTER XXV

Tink. Tink. Tink.

I opened my eyes to see the little trising flying around inside the glass bottle. It tried so desperately to get out.

Tink. Tink. Tink.

I felt sorry for it, a helpless little being trapped in such a small space. I wondered what its life was like, living in this forest and being so small. Malcolm had said they only come out at night. How did it survive with all the horrible creatures that Kenny mentioned? Was it just because it let off light that all the other creatures didn't bother it?

Malcolm was next to the trising, staring at the little creature. He looked as if he was in another place, staring off into the memories of his past. He used to live here, and after what I had seen, I wondered how he could have survived so long and what all he had dealt with.

"Is there something on my face?" he whispered.

I blinked. "What?"

"You keep staring at me. I thought maybe I had something on my face."

"Oh." I blushed. "You looked deep in thought, and I was just wondering what you could have been thinking about."

He gestured to come sit up next to him. I hesitated but decided if I sat by him, then we wouldn't wake anyone while trying to talk across the cave.

"I was thinking of what to do next," he whispered.

"And?" I asked.

"And I don't know. We can't stay in here forever. It's too dangerous. If we leave, we will probably be captured by Bill. We need to face Morpheus, but…"

"But I'm not ready for it?" I finished. It was exactly what I was thinking as well, and honestly I didn't know how I would ever be ready. I wasn't strong enough to face my fears. I was just a kid in high school. How could I do anything to face my fears?

"It's not your fault. Nothing in your world would have prepared you for this. You don't have people who can get into your mind like him."

I didn't think that was the truth; it was more than just that. "I know I'm weak, Malcolm. You don't have to sugarcoat it."

He shook his head. "No, even the strong fall under

Morpheus's influence. He has most of Wonderland under his thumb. It has nothing to do with being weak."

Tink. Tink. Tink.

I looked down at the little creature. It was trying its hardest to get out of the little cell it found itself in. "I feel sorry for it."

Malcolm let out a slight laugh. "Why?"

"Because it's in this scary world and it is so small."

"Trisings are monsters, demons really."

I looked at him, puzzled. "But it's so small."

He pointed at it. "Look at it. Do you see its fangs and claws? You think that kind of body is meant for sweetness?"

I looked closer. He was right. Instead of fingers, there were long claws, and as I brought my face closer, it opened its mouth as if it was hissing at me. Its mouth was full of sharp teeth, just like a shark's.

"Ew!" I backed away.

"You don't want to come across one of these in the middle of the night. They will tear your skin right off."

"That's morbid," I said.

He shrugged. "That's the Dark Forest. Everything here is morbid."

We sat in silence, and I imagined all the things that could be out there, waiting to kill us. Kenny had said that the creatures wouldn't come into the light. I tried not to think about that. *Stay positive*, I told myself, *you will get through this. You have a bunch of friends who would protect you.*

I glanced over at Malcolm, whose blinking seemed to get slower and slower. He was tired, especially after everything that had happened. Hell, he probably slept less than I had in the past few days.

"You can go sleep if you want. I'll keep watch," I said, straightening up as if I wasn't tired. Truthfully, I was.

He shook his head. "No, it's fine. You should sleep."

"If you want to protect me, then you need your strength. Go sleep."

He smiled. "Well, when you put it that way."

Moving over to what I guessed was a comfier spot, which seemed unlikely since everything was rock, he lay down and stared up at the ceiling. "If you need anything, just wake me up. Even if it's just to talk."

"Go to sleep already."

I watched as he shut his eyes. I kept an eye on him for a few moments before I decided he really was trying to sleep. Bringing my knees close to myself, I leaned my head on them and watched the trising trying to escape the jar.

Time passed as the others slept. I heard a few mumbles, as if someone was waking up, but whoever it was would just roll over and fall back asleep. Mainly that was Kenny. He was a very active sleeper, which didn't surprise me in the least.

"The Queen of Hearts, she made some tarts, all on a summer day; the Knave of Hearts, he stole those tarts and took them quite away," Kenny whimpered in his sleep. He was telling his story. Again.

They were tired; we were all tired. They'd put their lives on the line for me, and I wasn't going to wake them up from a sleep they all desperately needed.

"Alice ate the tarts, I swear," Kenny went on. I frowned. Well, maybe I would wake him up if I needed to. It was quite tempting, but he was loud and would probably wake the others.

It was strange that I wasn't cold in this cave. In the movies, if a person had to camp out in a cave, it always looked cold, but not here. It was always warm in Wonderland, which I was thankful for. There could be some slight chills, but that was it. It might have been moist in this forest, but at least I didn't have to suffer the coldness. Even being from Oregon, I hated the cold as much as someone from Arizona or something. It was just so miserable.

"Alice…," a voice called out from the distance. I had no idea who it was or where it was coming from.

I jolted up. "Who's there?"

The sound of a little girl laughing surrounded me. I just hoped it wasn't those flowers again. Or something worse. I glanced over at Malcolm, wondering if I should wake him up or not.

"You ask *far* too many questions. You're definitely Alice."

The voice sounded like a little girl. I looked around but saw no sign of whoever or whatever it was.

"Who or what are you?" I called out in a whisper.

"Silly Alice, can't you tell? I'm you." A form began to appear in front of me. It was me, or at least me when I was younger. She was a blonde in pigtails with a little blue dress and black shoes. I remembered that outfit; it was for the first day of kindergarten.

"That's not possible," I whispered. Well, it probably was. This was Wonderland after all.

She turned around and started skipping to the entrance of the cave. "Come on, Alice. We can go play. Don't you want to go play?"

"No, wait!" I ran after her into the darkness. Before I realized it, I was out of the cave. *Shit.* I spun around to find that I had already become lost. I couldn't see the entrance any longer.

"Crap, crap, crap!" I hurried back the way I thought the cave would be only to find more woods. "They're going to kill me." I gulped. "If something out here doesn't do that first."

The girl laughed. "Silly Alice, where are you going?"

"I want to go back to where I was," I answered, as if the little version of me was real.

"Why would you want to do that?"

"Because that is where my friends are."

"You don't need them. I'll be your friend."

Suddenly blue lights appeared on the ground, making a path. They twinkled in the darkness, only lighting up little parts of the path.

"This is the way you need to go, Alice. Come on! Let's play!" She appeared once more in the path, running and laughing.

I started after her. "Wait, where are you going?"

"Just trust in your friends, Alice. They will know where to take you. This way!" She giggled as she skipped.

More and more lights lit up before me. I couldn't see anything but the blue lights, like little bell-shaped figures. No trees, no stars, no plants, no creatures trying to kill me. Just the little blue lights and me as a little girl.

I hurried after her, but the faster I went, the farther she seemed from me. I had no idea what was going on, and I just wanted to be back with the others, but I had no idea where that was anymore. It was pitch-black other than the blue lights, and with the little girl looking like me, I had to know what it was and how it could do that. I still had my katana on me. I knew I would be fine. At least I hoped.

"That's it! Come on, Alice!"

The next step I took, I felt the rock give out. I screamed as I fell down. Quickly I grabbed the ledge and held on with all my might. The blue lights kept on, but I could now tell that below them was nothing. I was on the edge of a cliff, and the only thing below me was the never-ending pit of darkness.

"Let go, Alice. You never will know what's down there if you don't let go."

"Are you crazy? I'll die!" I exclaimed, my arm feeling as if it were going to give out. Why had I been so foolish to think that the girl would lead me to somewhere I needed to go?

"So?" She giggled.

I tried to pull myself up, but I felt the edge I was holding on to start to give way a little. I screamed as the dirt began to move under my hand.

Something grasped my arm, and I was forced back up onto the ledge. It was Malcolm.

"How did you—?" I began after he pulled me up on the safe ground.

He panted, out of breath. "I woke up and you were gone. Then I saw the blue lights and followed them."

I wrapped my arms around him. "Thank you. You saved me." I realized how close I was and backed away from him. I was a little embarrassed by that action.

"Don't ever do that again." He turned back the way he'd come. "We better hurry back before the lights disappear.

"It was me," I whispered.

"What?"

"The little girl, she was me. She brought me out here."

"It was probably a trickster. They will make you see what they want you to see. Then, as I found out, will send you over the edge."

I shook my head. "No, it was trying to tell me something."

"Tell you something?" he asked.

"Yeah," I smiled. "And I know exactly what we need

to do now to take down the circus."

CHAPTER XXVI

We were able to return to the cave before the blue lights completely disappeared. As we hurried back, I heard the little girl, the younger version of me, laughing and giggling. Nothing was worse than hearing oneself, especially when the apparition appeared right in front of them. It was creepy, actually, and I wished that it never would happen again.

But at least now I knew what I needed to do in order to defeat Morpheus. And it had been in front of me this entire time.

Malcolm and I sat back down next to the trising. It was apparent that he wasn't going to go back to sleep anytime soon. I wondered how much longer we had before it would be lights out or at least lighter.

All the others were still asleep, Kenny snoring away. I bet an earthquake could happen and he still would be asleep.

"What do you mean you know what we need to do next?" Malcolm whispered.

"Against Morpheus," I said. "I know how to beat him."

He shook his head. "How? How do you think you can beat him when just a little bit ago, you didn't even know what to do?"

"Alice showed me what I need to do."

"Alice?" He frowned. "You mean that trickster? They will tell you anything to kill you."

"Exactly, so we need to go to the circus as fast as we can. How do we get out of here?" I asked.

"We aren't going to the circus," he stated.

I looked at him in bewilderment, thinking at first he was joking. He wasn't. "Excuse me?"

"I'm not taking you there. I'm not risking it." He acted as if his decision was the only one that mattered.

I glared at him. "It's not your choice, Malcolm. We are going."

"Not without my help you aren't. You have no idea where these woods will lead you."

I moved closer to him. "Then help me. We have to beat Morpheus before it's too late."

He shook his head. "I don't want to put you through that again."

"It's not up to you; it's up to me. I know what I'm up against now, and I know what to do," I said sternly.

"And what's that?" he asked, his voice a bit louder.

"If I told you, then Morpheus will figure it out. I can't risk telling you. It will ruin the element of surprise."

He pinched the bridge of his nose. "How am I supposed to help you if you don't tell me what I need to do!"

"Just trust me. You'll know when the time comes!" I exclaimed. I hated being told what to do and was good at talking back. At least that's what my parents always said.

"You two sound like a married couple." Kenny yawned.

We both spun around to face him. "Do not!"

Kenny shrugged. "Whatever you say."

"She's being unreasonable. She thinks she can face Morpheus now, out of the blue," he said to Kenny.

I turned to him. "I'm right here. Why are you telling him like I'm not here?"

"Because you aren't listening to me!" he answered back.

Now he was starting to get on my nerves. I didn't understand why he couldn't just trust me. I knew what I was doing now. I had finally figured it out.

"What's going on?" A drowsy Davis started to get up. "Why is there yelling?"

"They are having a couple's spat." Kenny smiled.

We both glared at him. "We aren't a couple!"

He raised his arms in defense. "All right, all right. Just keep telling yourself that." He started to stand.

"But it's strange that you want to go to the circus all of a sudden."

"A trickster led her out in the dark." Malcolm stood up and stretched. "It tried to lead her off a cliff. Fortunately, I arrived before she lost her grip of the edge."

"A trickster? Are you sure?" Kenny asked.

"Yes," Malcolm answered.

"No, it was Alice. She was trying to show me how to beat Morpheus," I said. Everyone just stared at me.

"What did you say?" Chase was now up. "Alice?"

"The original Alice came to me to show me how to beat Morpheus. Well, I think it was the original Alice, but she appeared like me when I was a little girl. Either way, she showed me what to do."

"But she won't clue us in on exactly what that is," Malcolm added. "We just have to follow her lead and trust that this apparition is real."

Melvin yawned. "So are we going back there then?"

Malcolm and I locked eyes. I didn't turn away but held my own. I was going to win this fight and then I was going to win the fight against Morpheus.

He sighed and rubbed his face. "It's not a good idea."

"It's the only way to save Wonderland," I added. "This is the only way we're going to win."

Kenny stepped next to Malcolm and whispered something into his ear. Whatever it was, it made Malcolm even more angry, his eyes narrowing and hands clenching. He glared at Kenny for a moment but then looked defeated.

Malcolm sighed. "Fine, we will go."

I smiled in satisfaction. "Now how do we get out of here?"

"That will be the tricky part. We can't take a shortcut out to just make a portal there because Bill will find us and follow us. We can't make a portal out of here because the forest won't allow it. The only way to get out of here is to go through the heart of the Dark Forest and out the other side where the circus is located," Malcolm explained.

"How long will that take us?" I asked.

"At least three days if we don't run into any trouble," Kenny answered for him.

"So two more nights in this wretched place?" Davis groaned. "I want a real bed."

Chase stood up. He hadn't said a word about the circus and whether he agreed about going. I wondered what his thoughts were about it all. "Sun is rising. We should start moving now if we want to get out of here then."

I looked at the cave door and saw light, if you could really call it light, beginning to shine. It really was just not-as-dark-as-pitch-black light, but at least we could see each other out there. Malcolm grabbed the bottle with the trising.

"Well then, shall we?"

CHAPTER XXVII

We walked as fast as we could through the forest, trying to reach the other side. My heart pounded in my chest as trees around us cracked and moaned. I had just watched *Lord of the Rings* last weekend and became paranoid that the trees were going to get up and attack us even though the Ents aren't evil. In the real world, that would have been a silly notion, but here, anything was possible. And the fact a spider had tried to eat me the day before didn't help.

Letting the trising go was a scary experience. It wasn't completely light out, and it apparently didn't appreciate us capturing it for the night. The moment Malcolm let it out of the bottle, it attacked him and Kenny. I'll forever remember the sound of Kenny screaming. Never before had I heard a grown man scream like a little girl. Now the two of them had bite and scratch marks all over their arms. We must have run at least two miles before it was light enough for the creature to have to go back into hiding. It couldn't handle sunlight, which made sense to me. Creatures of Satan always hated sunlight in the movies.

After running for our lives, we got some food. I was very hesitant to eat it after everything that I had experienced here, but Kenny and Malcolm reassured me again and again that it was okay. They said they knew what was poisonous and what was not. I finally gave in, my stomach demanding something to eat.

What really concerned me was the random little signs inserted into the ground next to berries and plants that said Eat Me and Pick Me, et cetera. First off, who the hell posted those? Second, like hell am I going to believe those signs. I didn't believe anything in this forest, and I never wanted to come back. Ever.

Which probably meant, for some unforeseen reason, I would be back. That is if we got out of here in one piece.

A few hours passed, and we now found ourselves nearing the heart of the forest. The trees seemed to be getting denser, more creatures growled around us, and even more fog appeared to worsen our vision. I stayed close to Malcolm since he knew where he was going, and everyone else stayed close behind.

Melvin had his saber out, chopping down twigs and ivy so that we could pass. His arm had to have been getting sore after all the things he had to get rid of in our way. Davis switched out with him after a while, his claymore slicing right through everything just as the saber did.

A howling noise started echoing around us, and Malcolm took my hand to secure me next to him. I felt safe near him and closer after our fight. Even though I denied being a couple to Kenny, I really thought about the possibility. He had always been there for me, and I had a big crush on him in the real world. But here he was different. Here he was colder.

Or was that just a mask so no one could hurt him?

Then there was Chase. I enjoyed being with Chase. He was a good friend, but that was all I felt for him. Friendship. He was someone I could trust to be there even though together we ended up being trouble. What he felt toward me, I wasn't quite sure. It was all so complicated and not something I wanted to think about when first we had to take down the circus.

We stopped for a break. Melvin tapped a tree and got us all some water. Never did I feel so thirsty in all my life. Kenny grabbed some fruit and leaves, which he said were edible. I hoped he was right but trusted him after he found food for us earlier that didn't make me ill. We all ate our share and let our bodies restore its energy.

"How long did you two live out here?" I asked as we rested for a bit.

Kenny shrugged. "Oh, what, probably at least fifty years, give or take a few."

I gasped. "Fifty years?" That seemed impossible to have survived in a place like this for so long. I could barely handle the one day we were out here. They were strong and smart, I had to give them that.

"That's what happens when you go up against the Queen of Hearts," Chase explained. "She either cuts off your head or exiles you here."

"Did you get exiled here too?" I asked.

Chase laughed. "The queen could never catch me. I came here on my own sometimes. Get away from people. That's when I met Alice. She wandered in here on her own, looking for a path."

I turned to the others. "What about Melvin and Davis? How did you meet Alice?"

Davis started to open his mouth but didn't say anything.

"We were here as well, yes. We all met her here," Melvin answered.

"You were here in exile as well?"

"Yes, but not for that long. We had only been in here for a week or two," Melvin said.

"So maybe this forest is the key to beating Morpheus." I smiled.

"We just have to get out of here alive first," Davis whispered.

"Shouldn't be hard; you did it last time," I said.

"Yeah." Davis glanced at Malcolm and Kenny. "Barely."

I thought about furthering the conversation and

asking what he meant by barely, but I decided I didn't want to know. Between Malcolm and Kenny's bleak faces, I knew it wasn't a topic they wanted to press any further. I would figure it out someday though, if I had the chance.

After a few more minutes of silent rest, we started up again. The tension seemed to grow between the guys. Memories, I presume, from the last time they were here were coming back to them. No one said a word, but I could feel it and see it in the way they looked at each other.

Chase pulled me toward the back next to him as we made our way up a hill.

"Why are you sticking so close to him?" he asked.

I blinked, surprised at the question. It had come out of nowhere. "Because he knows this place the best."

"That's it?"

I nodded.

"Just be careful, all right? You don't realize how this place can affect a person. It might have been a long time ago, but Malcolm and Kenny used to rule these woods."

"What do you mean by rule?" I asked.

He started to say something, but out of the darkness, a loud roar rang through the trees. I spun forward to see one of the strangest creatures I had ever seen come out of the trees before us. Its head was round with large eyes and teeth that belonged on a tiger. Its long neck ran down to its round body and even longer tail. It had massive arms with claws that extended out toward us. Its dragon-like wings flapped vigorously to keep its body up off the ground.

It let out another roar.

Everyone pulled out their swords, even me. The beast charged at us, and everyone jumped out of the way. It screamed as Davis slashed it with his claymore. Angry, it grabbed the sharp edge of the sword with its claws out of Davis's hand and threw it. Davis just stared at it, horrified.

"Retreat!" Malcolm ordered.

We all ran to the right of it. It followed after us, making trees crash down beside it due to its large size.

Malcolm put his arm around me and guided me left. "This way, hurry."

Melvin and Kenny turned the other way, leading the creature away from us. Chase and Davis turned around and followed it.

"They are going to deal with it. I'm going to get you to safety." Malcolm pushed me farther away from the creature.

"No, we have to," I began when I felt him pull me back. All of a sudden we both started sliding down the cliffside. We both screamed as we tumbled onto the rocky ground below.

CHAPTER XXVIII

I don't know how long I lost consciousness, but when I woke, I found myself at the bottom of a cliff. Looking back up at where we had slipped, I couldn't believe I was still alive. My body ached from all the rocks beating against my body and twigs snagging my clothes and hair. After I caught my breath once more, I tried to stand.

My body didn't want to stand, or move really, and my leg was screaming at me in pain. It felt like it was screaming. It really did. I fell back down. "Ow…"

I peered around, looking for Malcolm. He was lying a few feet in front of me.

"Malcolm, can you hear me?" I whispered.

He didn't budge. I crawled over to him. He was completely knocked out. I tried not to panic, finding myself in a dire situation. I had to take deep breaths and calm myself down.

"Malcolm." I shook him. "Wake up, we have to get out of here. Wake up!"

Still nothing. I felt his wrist as we had been taught in Middle School health class and could feel a pulse. At least he was alive. A roar echoed behind me. I glanced back to see trees swaying back and forth. That creature was coming this way. I quickly turned back to Malcolm.

"Wake up! Malcolm! Please, for the love of…"

The monster roared again. I grabbed Malcolm's arms and pulled him in the opposite direction of where the sound was coming from. My leg exploded in pain.

"Please wake up. Please!"

The creature came flying through the trees, its scream piercing my ears. I didn't know if it was the same one as before, and if it was, I wondered where the others were.

I stayed still, hoping it couldn't see me like the T. rex in *Jurassic Park*, but that wasn't the case. It started flying straight for us.

Malcolm's eyes flickered open. "Oh, my head."

I pointed up. "Uh, Malcolm…"

"You have got to be kidding me." He tried to stand but failed. "I think my leg is broken. Alice, run! Get out of here!"

"I'm not going to leave you here."

"You will die if you stay here!"

I pulled out my katana. "No. You have saved me

multiple times. It's my turn."

I ignored the pain in my leg as I limped between Malcolm and the jabberwocky. The jabberwocky let out a fighting roar.

"No, I'll not let you hurt my friend! I'm sick of this place, and I'm not going to die by some stupid creature! I made it too far to die now!"

I charged at the creature, slower than I would have liked due to my leg. It dove at me, claws extended. The katana clashed with its claws. I spun forward and sliced one of its feet completely off. I got it right at the joint for a clean cut.

The creature screamed in agony. It looked mad, its eyes glaring at me. It wanted revenge and wasn't going to stop until it got it. It swooped down and attacked again, jaw open as if it would eat me right there. I jumped out of the way as its mouth came at me. I stabbed it straight in the eye. It screamed and collapsed on the ground, trying to make the pain stop. Quickly I swung the katana right through the creature's neck. The body fell along with its head, never to move again.

"Take that, you stupid, worthless piece of crap!" I yelled down at it. My adrenaline was high, and I'd had about enough of everything in this forest.

The fight must have been too much for my body as I suddenly collapsed.

"Alice!" Malcolm yelled.

I lay on the ground, staring up at the trees. Everything seemed blurry, like it was just one green mess. Maybe it was always like that. I didn't know. I just wanted to get out of there.

Where did I go wrong? What did I do in my life to deserve this? Getting kidnapped to a world that didn't exist? Then having to face my darkest fears and then taken into this wretched place? I just wanted to go home.

"Alice, can you hear me?"

My eyes flickered open. I had thought my eyes were open, but apparently that wasn't the case. I blinked a couple of times and found Malcolm leaning over me.

"You did it! You killed the jabberwocky." He smiled.

"I couldn't let it kill you, now could I? Who would save me when I need help?"

He laughed. "Thank you."

Malcolm stared into my eyes and I into his. It felt as if time had stopped for a moment as he leaned in closer and kissed me.

"Well, well, what do we have here?" Kenny's voice broke the magical moment. Malcolm backed away, and I saw everyone standing behind him. Chase was frowning. I blushed as I sat up. Apparently everyone was fine. That was great news.

"She killed the jabberwocky, no thanks to you guys. Where were you? Why didn't you defeat the jabberwocky like you were supposed to?" Malcolm tried to stand and collapsed once more. "Davis, get over here!"

Davis scurried over and knelt next to Malcolm.

"What happened?"

"We fell down the cliffside. I think my leg is broken," Malcolm explained.

Davis placed his hands over Malcolm's leg and closed his eyes. After a few seconds, he opened them again. "All good."

To my amazement, Malcolm stood up without a problem.

"What just happened?" I asked.

Davis hurried over to me. "I can heal people, Alice." Davis smiled as he placed his hands over me. "Just take a deep breath."

It hurt bad. I could feel my sprained ankle fix itself. I bit my lip in pain, not wanting to seem like a weakling. But God, it hurt.

"All done." He stood up and looked at the jabberwocky. "You did this?"

I nodded as I stood. "Yeah, I guess I did."

"Amazing!" Melvin came up beside me. "Not many people have gone against a jabberwocky and lived to tell the tale."

"We aren't out of this place yet, boys." Malcolm straightened his collar. "Now let's get a move on it."

Night finally came again, and I tried to sleep in the new cave we'd found, but too much was going through my mind. The jabberwocky, the kiss. Mostly just the kiss was what I kept thinking about. I didn't particularly want to think about the jabberwocky ever again. But the kiss, what did it mean? Was it just a yeah, we did it kiss? Or did it mean something more than that?

Chase was taking first watch. He sat near the entrance and stared out into the darkness. They had captured another trising and used it for light. This one put up less of a fight, which I was thankful for because it meant that it wouldn't try to kill us in the morning. At least that's what I hoped.

I went over and sat next to Chase. He didn't even glance at me.

"Couldn't sleep?" he asked.

"Nope. My body wants to, but my mind won't stop." I smiled.

"Thinking about that kiss?"

I couldn't believe he asked that. I looked down at the rocks beside my feet.

He spun around to face me. "What does he mean to you?"

"I… I don't know."

"You shouldn't like him. He isn't the man you think he is. He's cold and dark, and nothing can bring him out of that. Not even *you*."

Those words, they didn't describe Malcolm like I knew him. Malcolm had been kind since the moment I had met him. "What are you talking about? He's nice and sweet."

"If you knew him as well as I did, you would never say that. There's a darkness inside him that will never leave. That is why Morpheus can't affect him.

Malcolm's heart is much darker than that circus leader could ever imagine. But it's your choice. Just don't say I didn't warn you." Chase turned away.

I opened my mouth to say something but decided not to. I didn't want to gossip behind Malcolm's back. If I was going to find out about his past, I would ask him myself. Deciding to try to get some rest, I headed back to my spot and finally fell asleep.

Over the next two days, we made our way farther toward the circus. Never had my body been put through so much strain, not even in Becca's ballet classes. I was glad I was at least in shape to be able to walk so much even though my arms and legs begged me to stop.

Nothing major attacked us again, thankfully. A couple of small birds pecked at us, but Chase handled them like a pro. I wanted to comment on it, but after our conversation, we didn't really talk. Flowers around us sang, but at that point, we were used to their sweet lullabies.

At last I could see sunlight. It was setting in the distance, great reds and oranges making its way through the trees. I smiled.

"We did it. We're almost there," I said.

Kenny walked up next to me. "Now you will have to face Morpheus. You think you're ready?"

"Oh, after all that we have just gone through, I know I'm ready. Let's go."

By the time we got out of the forest, the sun had set,

and the stars and carnival lights lit up the area. It glowed spectacularly just as it did last time, looking innocent and charming to the unsuspecting eye. But I knew better. I knew the truth. It was dangerous and dark, and Morpheus would use any means necessary to get a person wrapped around his finger.

I wouldn't let him get away with it this time.

The moment we stepped through the entrance of the circus, I knew this would be an all-or-nothing mission. Either we were going to beat Morpheus once and for all or we would lose everything, and Wonderland would cease to exist. It didn't bother me, the weight of the mission on my shoulders, because I had the one thing that Morpheus didn't.

Friends.

Malcolm stepped up beside me. "Are you sure about this?"

"As sure as I'll ever be. Just trust me, okay? That's all that I ask of you," I said.

He nodded. "With everything I have to the very end."

I turned around to the other boys. "You all ready?"

They nodded.

I smiled. "Then let's bring this circus down once and for all."

The sound of clapping made me turn my head to find Morpheus approaching us. "I have to admit, Alice, I didn't expect to see you walking in here ever again."

"You don't frighten me anymore, Morpheus, just give up now." I stood tall, not letting my body admit fear.

He just laughed. "My dear, you're delusional. I would never admit defeat, and why would I need to? You could never conquer me. Not here. Not anywhere."

"That's where you're wrong. I have grown. I'm stronger, and I can defeat anything you throw at me."

Morpheus tilted his head. "Malcolm, are you going to let her destroy herself like this? You know I can take her to the point where not even you can bring her back."

"She won't need to be brought back," Malcolm said. "She's going to defeat you. I have no doubt in my mind."

He just smiled. "And I see you brought another friend. Kenny, isn't it? I remember looking inside your mind. There wasn't much there, now was there?"

Kenny stuck his tongue out at Morpheus.

"Well then, if you think you're ready, my dear child, I shall make the arrangements."

"The arrangements?" I didn't remember him having to plan for me last time.

"Yes, because this time you're going to be my main show." He tapped his cane. "Now come, my customers are waiting."

We followed him toward the tent, and a few of his workers joined us, making sure we weren't going to make a scene. I could tell Malcolm and the rest were nervous, but I didn't let their fear rub off on me. I had to stay strong because I knew exactly what I needed to beat Morpheus, and if I lost that, then I lost everything.

The tent was crowded once again with people from all over Wonderland. Their faces were all masked with darkness. I couldn't tell if they were enjoying themselves or not. I suppose they were since they were here. I wondered if they were in the ocean like I was when I was clouded in darkness or if each of them had their own special place.

"Ladies and gentlemen, boys and girls! Welcome to a show like no other! I'll be taking you to a place where none have gone before! Into the mind of my dear Alice here, a human from the real world. You will see the worries of those pathetic beings and see how much more advanced we are than them." Morpheus grinned. "And we will watch as she'll fall into my hands once more."

Grabbing my hand, he brought me into the center of the arena. The boys tried to come with me, but guards kept them back. Thousands of eyes stared down at me, and I felt my heart beat fiercely against my chest. It was just like a recital. All I had to do was my best.

Morpheus held up his hand, and fireworks filled the arena. "Let the games begin!"

CHAPTER XXIX

Everyone cheered as the fireworks went off, rooting for more. Jugglers and people with Hula-Hoops danced upon the tightwire, acrobats flung across the tent, and a unicyclist was eating fire while going around the arena. If this was a normal circus, it would have been spectacular.

But it wasn't a normal circus. It was evil, warped, and out to destroy the world, both mine and Wonderland.

The tent went dark. I could no longer see the crowd or the performers. It was happening; I would have to face my fears once again.

And this time I wouldn't give in.

All of a sudden my house appeared in front of me. It seemed worn down as if no one had been there in years. The windows were boarded, the paint was peeling, and weeds littered the yard in every direction. Not sure what was going on, I went and opened the door.

"Mom?" I called out into the house. "Dad?"

After stepping inside, I could tell for sure that no one had been there in years. All the pictures we had in frames were now shadows on the walls, and the furniture was torn to shreds.

I ran down the hall to my room and opened the door. All my paintings and belongings were still there. I quickly went and checked my parents' room and my sisters' room. There was nothing there. Why? How could that be possible?

"Mom! Dad!" I called out once again.

"They aren't there. They left." I could hear Morpheus's voice in my ear.

"Where are they?" I asked.

"Gone. They left you here. They couldn't stand being with you anymore, so they left," he explained.

They gave up on me? Why would they do that? I knew that they got mad at me, but in the end, they would always be there for me, *right?*

I had a big fight with them before I came to Wonderland. Would that have really made them mad enough to leave me? I would bring my grades back up, I promised that. Kate had said she would study with me. It was all going to be okay.

Because this wasn't real.

I shook my head. "They wouldn't do that. My parents would have never done that to me."

"But they're nowhere to be seen, Alice. They couldn't stand your bad grades or your attitude. You are a disgrace to them."

"No, my parents love me, and even though we don't agree, they know these are the things I want to do."

"They harp on you to stop wasting your time. You can't believe that they will support you in what you want to do."

"They may be hard on me, but that shows them I'm passionate in what I believe in. They will come around. They always do."

"Fine." Morpheus's voice sounded mad. "They may not leave you." The scene changed. I was now at school. There was no one in the hallways; everyone was either in class or at the gym. "But what about dear Kate?"

"Alice." Kate appeared in the hallway. She frowned when she saw me and stomped over. "Where have you been?"

"I… I don't know," I said.

"Well, never mind that. You are late and will probably receive another detention. That's the third one this week!" she exclaimed. "I don't know what has gotten into you, but you're turning into someone that I can't be friends with."

Detention? What the hell was going on? I mean, I have had a couple in the past due to being late but never that many in a week. "What do you mean?"

"I have straight As, Alice. You barely pass your

classes. I couldn't be friends with someone who always receives detentions all the time. It would ruin my reputation."

I shook my head. "Kate would never say that."

She put her hands on her hips. "Oh really? Then who am I?"

"You are my worst fear: the Kate that I hope will never come to be. The one who I fear will turn her back on me. But that is only a fear. I know for a fact that Kate would never leave me."

"Ugh, you're talking nonsense. You know, in reality, I should take your place. Your parents like me more than you anyway. You could just disappear, and no one would notice."

"Kate would never say that. She's my friend."

Her mouth turned up into a slight grin. "No one would notice."

"My best friend would never leave my side," I repeated again and again, letting it resound. "My best friend would never leave my side!"

The scene changed. I was no longer in the real world but in the Dark Forest. I had done it. I had successfully faced my fears of the real world. But why did I find myself here?

I stood alone. I could hear creatures move around me, and the fog was taking over the land. My heart began to beat faster. How was I in here? How did I get in this wretched place again?

And why was I here? Although this was a scary

place, it wasn't really a major fear of mine. So why was I here?

That's right; it was an illusion.

"Why are you all alone here, Alice?" Morpheus's voice echoed around me.

"I… I don't know."

"Your friends left you. They couldn't stand saving you any longer."

I shook my head. "No, they wouldn't do that. They wouldn't leave me."

"Take a look around, Alice. They aren't here."

"This is a trick. This isn't real. You should just give up now, I won't give in to my fears anymore."

"Not real, you say? Tell that to the creatures at your feet."

I looked down to see ten of the spider creatures that almost got me last time. I screamed and tried to kick them away.

"No one's here to save you. Just run, Alice. Run as fast as you can!"

I ran faster and faster into the woods. Twigs clawed at my skin, the blood running down my arms. More and more spiders seemed to join the chase. I wanted to call out for help, but I knew no one would be coming.

I went past the flowers singing the lullabies, the blue lights calling to me to run off the cliff, other lights in the distance that were probably those fairy things that wanted to kill me. I kept running nevertheless, as fast as I could manage.

Coming up to an opening, I stopped. I couldn't believe what I saw in front of me: a table covered in moss.

I found myself at the tea party once again.

I glanced behind me to find that all the terrors were gone. There was nothing following me any longer.

The only thing I could hear was the sound of my own breath as I slowly approached the table and chairs. Then I realized what was odd about all this—why it wasn't things that I feared in my dreams.

"I'm inside Malcolm's mind," I whispered.

"You are smarter than I give you credit for." Morpheus appeared in front of me. He looked as cocky as usual. "I didn't think you would ever figure that out."

"The spiders were Chase's fear; he was afraid of what would have happened if he didn't save me in time."

"Very good." Morpheus slid his fingers over the moss that covered the table. "Now you must be asking yourself, why is Malcolm afraid of this place? And more importantly, why is he afraid of you finding out?"

"I… I don't know."

"The answer is hidden away under all this moss." He smiled. "All you have to do is take it off, and all the answers will be given to you."

Slowly I took a step closer and placed my hand on the soft moss. I wanted to know what Malcolm was thinking. He had so many secrets that had been hinted at, that I had asked about, but no one gave anything away. I just wanted to know what could have been so bad that even Chase didn't trust him—things that the original Alice took him out of and helped him through.

Why did she get to know, and I didn't?

The moss would be easy to take away; it wouldn't take that much effort. I could just pick it up and be able to have all the answers revealed.

But I knew I couldn't.

I shook my head. "No, he is my friend! I would never do this to him!"

Morpheus appeared next to me and whispered into my ear. "He's hiding such darkness from you. Don't you want to know? Don't you have the right to know?"

"His past doesn't matter to me but who he is today. He's sweet and kind and cares about everyone! He cares about me!" I shut my eyes. "Friends trust each other, and I know they feel the same! My friends will always be here for me, and I'll always be there for them!"

I heard Morpheus scream as something threw him back. I opened my eyes to find myself on a beach. The waves gently came upon the shore.

"Where am I?" I whispered. "What is this?"

"Why, you are me," a young voice said behind me.

I turned around to find a young girl with long blond hair, smiling.

"Alice?"

She laughed. "That's me!"

"I don't understand."

"You realized the truth in yourself that Morpheus can't defeat. You realized not only how much power friendship has in your heart but how much power you have within." She pulled out a clear orb that shone brightly. "And with that, you will be able to save Wonderland." She handed me the orb. "This is the power of your heart. Use it well."

As quickly as I appeared, I was pulled back into the circus.

"You!" Morpheus pointed at me. "You ruined everything!"

He pulled a rapier out and charged at me. I started for my katana, but the clash of another sword hitting it distracted me. Malcolm and Chase stood between me and Morpheus.

"I don't think so." Chase grinned. "You are finished once and for all."

"Give up, Morpheus," Malcolm said as Melvin, Davis, and Kenny surrounded Morpheus. "Your reign is over."

Morpheus shook his head. "No, it will never be over."

He placed his sword back into his cane and slammed it against the ground. A puff of smoke engulfed him, and he was gone.

CHAPTER XXX

"He's gone!" Melvin waved the smoke away. There was no trace of Morpheus. The boys all turned to me, smiling.

Malcolm picked me up and spun me around. "You did it, Alice! You defeated him! He's running away with his tail between his legs. Ha!"

I blushed. "It was only because of you." I turned to the others. "Because of all of you. Your friendship led me to believe I could defeat anything. I knew you all would always be there for me, and I for you. Morpheus can control people by their fear, and I realized that having faith in not only my friends but myself, I could defeat anything."

Chase pointed at the orb. "What's that?"

"Oh." I looked down at the strange orb. I had almost forgotten about it. "Alice gave it to me."

Kenny held out his hand. "Let me see it."

I handed it to him, and he examined it. "If I'm not mistaken, this is the orb that got destroyed during the Red and White war."

"What?" Melvin exclaimed as he took it from Kenny. "This can't be it. I saw it get destroyed."

"What are you talking about?" I asked.

Malcolm grabbed the orb. "There was a powerful orb that the two kingdoms fought for. It was said to be able to bring all peace, or destruction, depending on who held it." He handed it to me. "Make your choice. Alice gave it to you."

I stared at it, not sure what to do with it. But, as if someone whispered the thought into my mind, I threw it at the ground, shattering it into thousands of little pieces. The moment it hit the ground, a flash brighter than any light I had ever seen went out into every direction. I jumped back, covering my eyes.

The light dimmed, and once my eyes finally adjusted, I looked around. Chase's eyes widened as the light came back to normal. Murmurs through the audience echoed in the arena.

"What was that?" Davis squeaked as he stood up.

"I don't know." Kenny's eyes narrowed as he peered around. He smiled. "Oho! Will you look at that!"

We all turned to see the audience staring at us. Staring. There was no longer darkness covering their face. We shouted in joy.

"We did it!" Melvin shouted. "We finally did it!"

Our joy ran short when Bill entered the arena. We all turned quiet when we noticed his face was also clear.

Malcolm stepped in front of him. "Bill."

Bill looked at us for a moment, then smiled. "We are free." He laughed and hugged him. "You sly dog, you did it!"

"Good to see you in a better mood," Malcolm said.

Melvin, Davis, and Chase went up to talk to Bill, but Kenny just stood next to me.

"Nice to see everything is back to normal," Kenny said.

"Yes." I watched as the others talked to Bill. "But Morpheus is still out there."

"He has no power now, not after you broke that orb. I still don't understand how you got it, but I'm sure happy you did."

"Alice gave it to me. She must have known you all would have needed it later." I laughed. "This place is so strange; it makes no sense. But I like it. It's a breath of fresh air away from reality."

"So the question is." Kenny looked at me through the corner of his eye. "Where are you going to go next?"

I looked back at Malcolm and the others. I'd forgotten I would have to go back, away from this place. I worried about home and being gone, but I never thought about having to leave this place. Truth was, I loved it here, now that people weren't after me. This place could be nice, especially with my new friends.

"Alice," Chase called. "Come on, we need to leave."

I hurried over. "What do you mean?"

"We have to report all this to the king and queen, of course," Bill said. He glanced at Kenny, a little grin appearing on his lips. "Now that you have saved us."

Chase grabbed my hand, and suddenly we were in front of the palace. I could appreciate the beauty of it better now that I didn't have to worry about my head getting chopped off. Paper lanterns hung in space all around us. A figure came running out toward us.

"Alice!" the queen called. "Malcolm, you did it!"

Malcolm and the others bowed in front of the queen.

"All as expected for the queen's head servant," Malcolm said.

"You will be heavily rewarded." She looked at us all. "All of you."

"Thank you, Your Majesty." Malcolm bowed again.

"As for you." The   queen stepped in front of me. "I don't know how, but you defeated Morpheus and restored Wonderland. How will I ever repay you?"

"Oh." I blushed. "I don't want anything in return. It was these boys that did everything, really."

She smiled. "Oh, I'm sure you handled a great deal of it. This group never have been able to work together before."

"Really?" I asked. "That's surprising."

"You must be one amazing girl." She winked. "Now, shall we head inside?"

We nodded and followed the queen inside. This time I was able to really relax as I strolled through the palace with the others. It was still as magnificent as when I entered the first time, and it was a relief to be able to see the faces of everyone who passed. They all smiled at us, bowing thanks as they went on with their work. It felt great to have done something for others, and even if I wasn't given praise like this, I still would have done it.

As we went farther down the corridors, something caught my eye and I stopped. Everyone kept forward as I peered down the adjacent corridor. A small figure stood in the distance. The White Rabbit.

Without thinking, I followed him. Once he saw me heading to him, he turned around and started running. I ran after him. I don't know what the driving force was that caused me to do that, but I did. I ran after him. Maybe it was just curiosity.

He disappeared around a corner, and once I made it around it, he was gone. There was only one door at the end of the hall. I stepped to it, slowly, my mind only focusing on the door.

I slid it open to find the only thing in the room being a mirror. It was large, elegant. I had never seen something so beautiful. Standing in front of it, I heard the door shut behind me. I spun around to see the White Rabbit.

"You aren't supposed to still be here, Alice. You are supposed to leave," he said.

"What do you mean?" I backed away from him.

"Goodbye, Alice." He shoved me and I fell back.

CHAPTER XXXI

My eyes opened, and I found my TARDIS alarm clock wheezing and groaning. I pushed the top of it and turned it off. The smell of oil paint filled my nostrils. I looked around, confused. My paintings were scattered across the room, and dirty clothes were in piles all over the floor.

I was home.

I rubbed my eyes and tried to remember what had happened. Wonderland. *No, that couldn't have been possible.* I shook my head. *It was a dream. It had to have been a dream.* There were too many fumes in my room. I should probably air it out in here.

Rolling over, I brought the covers over my head, letting the warmth protect me. It couldn't have been real. It was ridiculous.

But something in the back of my mind kept saying it

was.

I finally pulled myself out of bed and got ready for the day. I was to meet Kate downtown, and we were going to go shopping. I wanted to get my mind off my recent grades, but for some reason it didn't bother me like it did last night. Maybe it had to do with my dream or whatever it was.

My mom dropped me off near Nordstrom's, and I hurried inside. The rain was coming down hard now, and I hated the feeling of wet clothes, especially when it was really cold out as well. The dampness reminded me of my dream. The Dark Forest was always damp, but at least it wasn't cold. I shook the thoughts out of my head. *It wasn't real. What was I thinking?*

I found Kate near the Free People section and hurried over to her. After our usual hug, she looked at me. "You look different, Alice."

I raised an eyebrow. "Is that a good thing?"

She smiled. "Yes, you look more confident."

"Actually, I feel a lot better. I had a fight yesterday with my parents, but for some reason I woke up feeling refreshed."

We spent the rest of the day looking through clothes and eating lunch at the Golden Crown, then finished up the afternoon going through the antique store that we swore a ghost lives in. We even stopped by the comicbook store that carried high-class signed comics, one in particular I liked that I wished I could afford. A Stan Lee signed *the Amazing Spider-Man*, the first introduction to Dr. Connors, aka Lizard Man. Only a couple thousand dollars, that's all.

Kate's mom picked us up, and we ate dinner at Christo's, a nice little pizza and pasta place. Then we retired back to her house and watched, ironically, Syfy channel's *Alice*. It was Kate's pick, not mine.

As we watched the three-hour-long miniseries, we came upon the jabberwocky.

I threw a piece of popcorn at the TV. "That's not what the jabberwocky looks like."

Kate gave me a look. "What did you say?"

"That's not what it looks like."

"It's a creature from a fairy tale. How would you know what it looks like?" she asked.

I shrugged. "I don't know. I just do."

"You are silly, Alice."

We finished the series and ended up having a *Teen Titans* marathon. Sunday went by as well, and we finished up homework that was due that Monday. Kate's mom dropped me back off at home, and after proving to my parents that I had finished my homework and Kate reassuring them it was perfect, I went into my room and painted.

I painted what I remembered from the dream: the Dark Forest, the Kingdom of Dreams, the circus. I decided to use watercolors for each of them and opened my window to get the lingering oil paint smell out of my room. It never seemed to leave. Once I was finished, I used a hairdryer to make sure the colors were as deep as I wanted them, then finally went to bed.

Monday morning came, and I got to school and emptied my bag in my locker, the books making a loud thunk as I shoved them on the top shelf. Kate stood by, all ready to go to first period.

"Oh look, Alice! It's your boyfriend." She poked fun at me as she did every day.

I glanced over to see Malcolm and the others putting their books away as well. Malcolm looked over and I blushed.

"He's not my boyfriend. You know that."

"But your cheeks get so red when I say things like that." She laughed.

I shut my locker and started for class. "You are so mean, Kate."

As we were almost to our room, I felt someone's hand on my shoulder. Turning around, I found Malcolm standing right behind me.

"After all that we have been through, you don't even say hi to me?" He smiled.

I stared at him for a moment, thinking. No, it couldn't have been real. Chase, Melvin, and Davis came up behind him. I grinned and flung my arms around Malcolm.

"It was real!" I laughed. "And you came back!"

"Of course we did. You didn't think we would leave our favorite girl behind, do you?" Chase grinned.

"Um, Alice," Kate said as she saw my arms around Malcolm. "Did I miss something?"

"No, you missed nothing at all."

"Okay." She pointed down the hall. "But you do see those girls running toward you as if they're going to attack."

I quickly ducked into the classroom, happy to know my friends were still with me and everything hadn't been just a dream. Chase and Davis sat next to me along with Kate. I smiled, happy to have such great friends in my life.

With them, I knew I could overcome anything.

Thank you so much for reading! Readers like you make it possible for authors like me to write stories! If you could spare a moment and leave a review on Amazon, Goodreads, BookBub, and wherever you like to buy books, that would mean the world to me! It really helps authors like me to succeed in the publishing world.

Book 2 coming out December 8, 2020!

Acknowledgements

I want to thank everyone who made this novel possible. A big thank you to my editor Justin Boyer who hopefully hasn't gotten sick of reading my stories yet. Thank you to Biserka Designs for the amazing covers they have done for my books. And lastly, thank you to my husband and parents who are always supporting me.

About the Author

Dani Hoots is a science fiction, fantasy, romance, and young adult author who loves anything with a story. She has a B.S. in Anthropology, a Masters of Urban and Environmental Planning, a Certificate in Novel Writing from Arizona State University, and a BS in Herbal Science from Bastyr University.

Currently she is working on a YA urban fantasy series called Daughter of Hades, a YA urban fantasy series called The Wonderland Chronicles, a historic fantasy vampire series called A World of Vampires, and a YA sci-fi series called Sanshlian Series. She has also started up an indie publishing company called FoxTales Press. She also works with Anthill Studios in creating comics through Antik Comics.

Her hobbies include reading, watching anime, cooking, studying different languages, wire walking, hula hoop, and working with plants. She is also an herbalist and sells her concoctions on FoxCraft Apothecary. She lives in Phoenix with her husband and visits Seattle often.

Feel free to email her with any questions you might have!

danihootsauthor@gmail.com